"I'm going to have to get to know you all over again...."

"You may not like me," Amy said.

Michael's golden gaze held warmth and humor. "I already like you. You're my wife. I married you."

She bit her lip. "But you don't remember that."

"True, but I have enough confidence in myself to know that I must have married you because—" he paused fractionally "—because I was passionately in love with you. Don't tell me it's not true. Don't tell me I married you because of your money, or that I won you in a poker game or...."

Amy managed a shaky smile. "No, no. We got married for all the right reasons."

Michael heaved a sigh of relief. "Good. Well, then, we have nothing to worry about. I'll just fall in love with you all over again."

Nothing to worry about. How wrong he was.

Ever since **KAREN VAN DER ZEE** was a child growing up in Holland, she wanted to do two things: write books and travel. She's been very lucky. Her American husband's work as a development economist has taken them to many exotic locations. They were married in Kenya, had their first daughter in Ghana and their second in the United States. They spent two fascinating years in Indonesia. Since then they've added a son to the family as well and lived for a number of years in Virginia before going on the move again. After spending over a year in the West Bank near Jerusalem, they are now living again in Ghana, but not for good!

Karen van der Zee

A WIFE TO REMEMBER

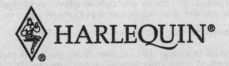

HARLEQUIN®

TORONTO • NEW YORK • LONDON
AMSTERDAM • PARIS • SYDNEY • HAMBURG
STOCKHOLM • ATHENS • TOKYO • MILAN • MADRID
PRAGUE • WARSAW • BUDAPEST • AUCKLAND

ISBN 0-373-18744-0

A WIFE TO REMEMBER

First North American Publication 2000.

Copyright © 1999 by Karen van der Zee.

CHAPTER ONE

HE DID not know this man, but one thing he knew for sure: he didn't like his face.

It was handsome enough, he supposed, with strong features and a confident chin—nothing objectionable, really—but there was something about the expression that frightened him and irritated him at the same time.

He looked older than he had expected, his expression weary. Deep grooves ran by the side of his mouth and his eyes looked tarnished.

Michael tried to read the character, the state of mind, to find at least something there of humor and lightness, but the face offered him only a bleakness that was disconcerting.

What was wrong with this face, with this man? Something dark and tormented lay hidden in the shadows. He didn't know what or why. It was the face of a man who had no hope, no illusions.

Michael stared at his reflection and felt a flash of exasperation.

"Good heavens, man," he muttered to himself. "You're alive! Smile!"

He smiled.

In the mirror the face smiled back.

"All right," Michael muttered, studying himself. "That's better."

The phone shrilled in her ears as Amy entered her apartment and annoyance instantly rushed through her. She'd spent three weeks away from civilization and the first thing she had to hear was the blasted telephone. Well, she had no intention of answering it.

She hauled her heavy backpack into the bedroom, took off her battered hiking boots and began opening windows.

The ringing stopped. Good. She pulled her T-shirt over her head and stripped off her jeans. Now for a long, luxurious shower. Ah, bliss!

The phone began to ring again, insistent, desperate.

She fled into the bathroom, ignoring it.

Half an hour later she was in the kitchen heating a frozen pizza when the wretched phone began to shriek again.

Capitulating, she picked it up. "Hello," she said with a note of resignation.

"Amy? Is that you? Oh, I'm so glad you're there!" A female voice, high, nervous, desperate. "I've been trying for weeks to get hold of you! Oh, Amy—" The woman broke into weeping.

Amy's heart turned over. She recognized that voice. It belonged in the past, the past she'd tried to leave behind, but with which she still struggled in dark, agonizing moments.

"Melissa!" It was all Amy could say. A mixture of conflicting feelings overwhelmed her. She liked, loved Melissa, but Melissa was too close to the place in her soul where she didn't want to be.

"Amy, oh, Amy! Something terrible has happened and I'm so sorry to call you but I didn't know what else to do! I'm having a baby and I have to stay in bed and I can't go anywhere—''

A baby. Melissa was having a baby. Amy swallowed and sat down on a chair. ''Melissa! What's wrong? Why do you have to stay in bed?''

''I had some problems and I was in the hospital and now I can't get out of bed until the baby is born, but that's not why I'm calling. Oh, Amy...I...'' More sobbing. More unfinished sentences, barely understandable.

''...somebody's got to go and help him and you're the only one...I'm so sorry. I know this is not fair—'' Melissa's weeping was distressing to hear.

''Melissa, please, please, tell me, what is it? Who are you talking about?''

''Michael,'' Melissa sobbed. ''He was in a car accident, a car of drunk teenagers—''

Michael. Car crash. Amy grew cold as terror seized her. No, she thought. Oh, please, no.

''Michael?'' She squeezed his name out on a terrified breath. ''What's wrong? How bad is it?''

''It's his head, I mean, he's all right physically except a broken arm, but—''

''His head?'' Horrible visions flashed through her mind.

''They can't find anything wrong, but he doesn't know faces and people anymore. I called him and he didn't know who I was!'' Melissa cried. ''I mean, they'd told him I was his sister, but when I talked to him he didn't know me and it was so awful, like talking to a stranger!''

''Where is he?'' Amy asked, her voice sounding

odd in her own ears, disembodied. Was he still on the island?

"He's in Oregon. He has a new job managing a fancy resort on the coast. He'd just got there a few days before the accident. Nobody even knows him there, Amy! Nobody! He's all alone!"

Amy stared blankly at the wall. Michael had moved away from the island in the Caribbean where he'd been the manager of a luxury resort, away from the house they had shared, the house she had furnished and decorated with love.

"I told him to come to Boston," Melissa was saying, "and stay with me and Russ, but he says he doesn't want to impose and that he has a job to do and he'll be fine."

More distraught weeping. "I'm his only sister! Russ is his best friend! How can he be *imposing*? But then I guess he doesn't know me from Adam and I'm just a stranger and…oh, Amy, will you go to him?"

Amy forgot to breathe, felt a suffocating sense of panic.

"Please," Melissa pleaded. "You're the only one. I wouldn't ask, it's just…I can't go. I have to stay in bed or I'll lose the baby. And Russ won't leave me by myself. Oh, Amy, I know it's not fair to ask you!"

No, it wasn't fair.

It was a nightmare even to contemplate it.

Amy closed her eyes, trembling with fear and horror and a whole mishmash of emotions. *I can't do this!* she thought. *Please, God, I can't do this!*

"I'll go to him," she heard herself say.

* * *

Amy pulled out a suitcase from the closet and started tossing in clothes, trying not to think. She'd called the airline and reserved a seat on a flight leaving midday tomorrow.

Pushing aside some assorted junk on the top shelf in the closet, she found a blue plastic storage container and deposited it on the bed. She snapped the lid open. Photo albums. She selected several, including a white one with gold lettering. *"Your Wedding Album"*, it said. She tucked them in with her clothes. Glancing back into the container, she reached for the package wrapped in a white plastic shopping bag and hid it quickly underneath her jeans in the suitcase. She noticed her hands trembling.

She got ready for bed, then lay staring up at the ceiling, wide-eyed and sleepless.

Michael had been in an accident. Michael had amnesia.

Don't think. Don't feel.

If she gave her thoughts and feelings free rein right now, she'd never get on that plane tomorrow.

Amy sat in the plane, feeling imprisoned, knowing there was no escape now. She hadn't seen Michael in two years. Two years of trying to forget, to accept that the fairy tale of her life with him had ended in tragedy.

And now she was on her way to see him again, to find out if she, the woman he had once loved, was able to help him get back his memory. And if she succeeded, if he remembered again, he would remember too that terrible morning, when their fairy tale had turned into a nightmare.

For a fraction of a moment she felt a perverted

sense of envy. *Michael didn't remember anymore. Michael was lucky.*

Right before the plane landed she took a small box out of her purse and opened it. The diamond sparkled up at her, taunting. Her hand trembled as she took the ring out of the box. *Don't think. Don't feel.*

She slipped it on her left ring finger.

It didn't take long for her to find him. He was tall and broad-shouldered, towering out over a good number of the people milling around in the arrivals lounge. Her heart lurched and her knees turned weak as she watched him—this man who had once swept her off her feet, this man she knew so well. It suddenly hurt to breathe.

He was searching the crowds for her, then glancing back at something in his hands. A photo. Melissa had sent him a picture of her last night, or Russ had, at his office, by some fancy computer scanning device.

Again his gaze swept around, passing over her without recognition.

He didn't know her, not even with a picture in his hand.

My hair, she thought suddenly. The photo had to be several years old and would show her with long hair. Last year she'd cut it short and it gave her a totally different look.

She forced herself to move toward him, her legs feeling stiff and wooden. He was wearing jeans and a loose black shirt and he carried his left arm in a sling. He looked thinner than she remembered him, his lean face gaunt and more sharply defined. Older.

It was the face of a man who hadn't smiled much
lately. There was some gray in his dark hair at the
temples which hadn't been there before.

"Michael?" Her heart hammered against her ribs.

"Amy?" No recognition in his brandy-colored
eyes.

She nodded, unable to make a sound, staring at
him, transfixed.

Surprisingly, there was a spark of humor in his
eyes. He smiled at her. "You're my wife, my sister
told me."

It was a lie. She was not his wife, not anymore,
but Melissa had told him that, afraid his pride would
not allow Amy to come if he knew they'd been divorced now for a year, knowing he would not want
charitable actions from people who were strangers
to him now, and certainly not from an ex-wife.

She nodded, knowing she had to do something
wifely, something loving.

She had to put her arms around him and kiss him.

Blindly she took a step forward, reached for him,
put one arm carefully around his neck, her cheek
against his. She felt his cast against her breasts,
smelled the clean, manly scent of him—intimately
familiar, as if only yesterday she had been in his
arms.

His right arm came around her back, holding her
gently.

From some deep reservoir, a tidal wave of grief
and longing surged over her, unstoppable.
Terrifying.

No, she thought, *please, no.*

With her face pressed against his warm cheek, her

body began to shake with sudden anguished sobbing.

"It's all right," he said soothingly, his hand stroking her back. "We'll work it out."

Work out what? she wanted to ask, but she had no words, only tears as she stood there in his arms. She struggled to gain control over her wayward emotions and straightened away from him, from this man who was so familiar yet so strange, this man who did not know her.

She fished in her purse for a tissue. "I'm sorry," she said shakily.

He regarded her with the eyes of a friendly stranger. "Nothing to be sorry for," he said easily.

She mopped at her eyes, blew her nose. "You really don't recognize me, do you?"

He shook his head slowly. "No," he said quietly. "I'm...sorry."

It hurt more than she could have ever imagined, to not be recognized by Michael, to be a...*nobody* to him, the man she had once loved with all her heart and soul. New tears blurred her vision.

"Don't cry," he said, "please don't cry." There was an odd unsteady tone in his voice. She blinked away her tears, looked into his eyes. The glimmer of humor had died, had been replaced by a strangely haunted look full of dark coppery shadows.

She swallowed miserably. "I'm sorry," she whispered.

"I'll be all right, you know. I'll be fine." He took her hand. "Let's go."

A car with a driver was waiting for them. Michael sat down next to her in the back seat. He couldn't drive himself, Amy realized, not with his arm in a cast.

"Melissa didn't tell me you had your hair cut," he said. "I was looking for long hair."

"She hasn't seen me since I cut it," she said, which was the truth. "May I see the picture she sent you?"

He plucked it out of the breast pocket of his shirt. It was a wedding photo—the two of them, cheek to cheek, ready to cut the wedding cake. The two of them laughing, looking so young and carefree, so radiantly happy.

Another lifetime. Another reality.

"I like this picture," he said, giving a half-smile. "We look quite deliriously in love."

She glanced back down at the picture. "Yes," she said, steeling herself against the onslaught of emotions. They had no longer been happy by the time she had left him. He had no longer been the man she had married. The photo portrayed a life that was forever lost. She handed it back.

"I must have had a picture of you in my wallet, but it was in my suit jacket and was burned in the car," he said. "At least that's what they think, because I wasn't wearing a jacket and I had no identification on me."

He had not had a photo of her in his wallet, she was sure. Melissa had told her that Michael had miraculously managed to crawl out of the car before it went up in flames, and that it had taken ages to figure out who he was, the search complicated by the fact that the car Michael had been driving was on loan and the owner had been out of the country.

Amy shivered. "It must have been horrible."

"On the bright side, I don't remember it," he said, and she caught the dry humor in his voice.

She stared at him. "Michael..."

He gave a wry smile. "Much as I want my memory back, I assume that like everyone else I have things in my life I'd just as soon not remember."

Amy felt her body tense. "Unfortunately, we don't generally have a choice in the matter," she said, managing to sound calm.

"No," he said evenly, "we don't."

The ride along the rugged Pacific coast was beautiful, but she was too nervous and overwrought to enjoy the spectacular scenery. She caught herself staring at Michael, who kept looking at her with a curious expression.

He was probably wondering how to act with a wife he didn't remember, or how he could have possibly chosen her for a wife. Did he like what he saw? Was he attracted to her at all?

"Melissa sent me a slew of family photos," he said. "Of our parents and our childhood, vacation shots, my graduation pictures, things like that."

"She told me they didn't help."

"No. It was like looking at someone else's photos, except I could tell by the resemblance that I was the kid in the pictures."

She glanced at his face, not able to imagine what it would feel like to not recognize yourself on photos. "It must feel so strange, not even to remember yourself," she said.

His mouth quirked at the corner. "I'm not sure how good it would be to remember myself as a kid. I looked like I wasn't up to much good in most of

the shots, and from what Melissa told me I was quite
a hellion."

"I know some of those stories." She managed a
half-smile, then again glanced out the window. She
wasn't sure what to say to him, where to begin. She
glanced back over at him again. "Does your arm
hurt?"

"No, not anymore. My ribs are more of a problem, but they're getting better too. Sleeping is difficult." He gave a crooked little smile. "I'm not
complaining. I'm alive, and I'm grateful for that."

It was a miracle he had not suffered more serious
injuries. It was a miracle he wasn't dead. Another
shiver ran down her spine.

"Melissa told me you spent the last month rough-
ing it in the Appalachians," he went on. "Wilder-
ness camping with a group of high-school kids."

She nodded. "Yes. I do it every summer. I didn't
know this had happened to you. Melissa didn't know
where I was and she didn't reach me until I got to
my friend's house in Philadelphia. I came as soon
as I could." She had practiced this little speech in
her mind.

He scrutinized her for a silent moment. "You
don't seem like the type who roughs it easily."

His words surprised her. "I don't?"

"You don't look very...tough. As a matter of fact
you seem rather fragile."

"I'm not fragile," she said. "We did a lot of
climbing and hiking on the island."

He frowned. "Did we? We must have photos
somewhere, in our shipment from the island."

"Yes." If he hadn't thrown them all out. Well,

she had the ones she had brought from Philadelphia. "When is the stuff coming?"

"I spoke to the moving company yesterday and they said it will be delivered the day after tomorrow." He gave her a quick smile. "Then we can move into the house. It's a great place, up on the cliffs with a view of the ocean and woods in the back. I hope you'll like it, but if you don't we'll find another one."

"I'm sure I will." It didn't matter if she did. She wouldn't really live there for any length of time. School would start again in a few weeks; she'd have to be back in Philadelphia by then.

A large wooden marker indicated they had arrived at the Aurora Nova Resort Hotel. The car slowed and turned onto a shady road that wound lazily through the woods. Melissa had told her that Michael was living in a suite at the hotel, waiting for his personal belongings to arrive from the island.

The car stopped in front of the main building. Michael took her hand as they entered the spacious lobby, all hardwood and field stone and natural light. "At least we are not one of these couples who have nothing to say to each other," he said, guiding her into an elevator. "You'll have to fill me in on my entire lifetime of misdeeds. According to Melissa, that might take a while."

They got out on the third floor. Michael took out a card and slid it into a door and opened it, stepping aside to let her in ahead of him. It was a cozily furnished sitting room, she noticed, no beds in sight. A teenaged kid, all tan and muscle, was right behind them with her two suitcases and Michael directed him to put them down in the bedroom to the left.

There was another door to the right, but it was closed. Was it another bedroom?

She'd been mulling over the sleeping arrangements, what to tell him, how to handle them. Being a loving wife, surely she could not ask for her own bedroom? Could she come up with some sort of reason or excuse?

"I haven't slept well since the accident," he said, gesturing at his arm in the cast. "I thought you might be more comfortable in your own bedroom for the time being, just so I won't bother you tossing around and getting up in the middle of the night."

Well, that took care of that. She felt an odd mixture of relief and pain. "If you think it's best." She wondered if his concern for her was real or if it was merely that he didn't want to share a bed with her, because, after all, he did not know her. The cast was a handy excuse.

"If you're tired," said Michael, "we can get the restaurant to bring us a meal up here. I know it's three hours later for you. But we can go out if you'd rather. The restaurant here is excellent and it has a nice ambience."

It would be much easier to be in a public place, she thought. "I wouldn't mind at all having a civilized meal served to me at a table, actually. I've been living on freeze-dried survival rations the last few weeks."

He grimaced with distaste. "Then we'd better get you some real food. A good steak or something."

"I'm a vegetarian," she said. "So are you." Well, at least she'd tried to make him one when they'd been married.

His brows arched in surprise. "I guess that's one

more thing I don't remember. I've been eating meat ever since the accident. Love the stuff.''

"It's bad for you,'' she said, unable to resist. "It's full of hormones and chemicals and fat and cholesterol.''

"Okay, no steak for you," he said easily. "You have whatever strikes your fancy. What time would you like to go? How about in an hour? That'll make it eleven for your body clock; are you sure it's not too late?''

"It'll be fine. I don't feel tired." She was much too keyed up.

"All right, then. I'll leave you to get unpacked and settled. I have a few things to see to at the office but I won't be long.''

She had a shower and shampooed her hair. Getting rid of all the airplane smells made her feel better. What to wear? She hadn't brought much in the way of dress clothes, so the choice was easy. Her old standby would have to do—a simple black shift that could be dressed up or down with jewelry depending on the occasion. She pulled a string of amber beads over her head, matching them with amber earrings. She'd take her soft, multi-colored jacket in case it was chilly.

She studied herself in the mirror, judging herself a bit thin and scrawny, but that was nothing new. It was nice to wear a dress again, to feel feminine again.

Dressed and ready, she left her room. Michael had returned and was standing in the open door to his bedroom. He was barefoot, trousers on, his shirt unbuttoned. Her pulse leaped as she glimpsed his broad, tanned chest, so wonderfully sexy with the light covering of dark hair. He gazed at her for a long silent moment, his eyes darkening.

"You...look beautiful," he said.

She felt strangely breathless. "Thank you."

"I wonder...would you mind helping me for a moment?" he asked. "Would you put my belt through the loops? It hurts my ribs to reach back."

"Of course, sure." She rushed over to him, took the belt from him and quickly slipped it through the loops of his waistband. He was trying to button his shirt with his good hand, making slow progress.

"Here, I'll do it."

He was gazing down into her face and she was too close, much too close to him. She focussed on the small buttons, fastening them, her hands trembling.

"You smell nice," he said softly.

So do you, she wanted to say, but the words stuck in her throat. She had always loved his warm, male scent, uniquely his. She'd always loved putting her face against his chest, or in the crook of his neck and breathing it in.

She had to get away from him. This was crazy. She couldn't allow herself to feel this way. She no longer loved this man. He had hurt her beyond measure. He did not love her. They were strangers to each other in more than one way, beyond amnesia.

She took an unsteady step away from him. He was trying to push his shirt into his trousers but he couldn't reach back and there was only one thing to do. Like an automaton she tucked in his shirt in the back, and he zipped up his trousers and buckled his belt by himself. He reached for a tie that had been knotted already and slipped it over his head and she tightened it and straightened the shirt collar, never looking at his face.

"When is the cast coming off?" she asked.

"If all goes well, in two weeks."

"Who's been helping you get dressed the last few weeks?" She tried to sound businesslike.

"The hotel masseuse comes by every morning. She doesn't know how to tie ties, so my secretary does that if I need to wear one, and she got this one ready to go."

Amy said nothing. The hotel masseuse and his secretary. She hoped they weren't fighting over him.

"It's not in their job description, so I'm grateful they're helping me out," he added evenly.

She knew that tone. He was trying to get a response from her, teasing her as he had used to do, long ago.

"You're a lucky man," she said sweetly.

"You're not jealous?" he asked, sounding quasi wounded. "Wives are supposed to be jealous in this sort of situation."

"Not me," she said lightly, finally meeting his gaze.

His mouth curved in a smile. "I like you better by the minute," he said.

How could a man forget a woman like her? Michael asked himself. Huge green eyes, a soft, kissable mouth, pale, reddish gold hair, freckles on her nose. No classical beauty, but she had a feminine allure that reached out straight to the male in him.

A month ago they'd still lived on St. Barlow. He had no recollection of the island, the house, the resort hotel he had managed, the wife he had loved.

Only weeks ago this woman had been sleeping in his bed; how could he possibly not remember touching her, stroking her body, making love to her?

He closed his eyes. What craziness had happened to his brain, his mind? How was this possible?

All he had to do was look into her clear green eyes and he wanted to lose himself in them. All he had to do was look at her and know that loving her would be the easiest thing in the world to do.

But he didn't know her. And he didn't remember loving her.

And she was his wife.

CHAPTER TWO

THE elevator was empty, bright and gleaming, sporting tinted mirrors on three sides. Michael stepped back to let Amy enter, then followed her in, frowning as he glanced at his own reflection.

Amy observed him. With his thick dark hair, his strong features and his chin jutting out slightly, he was a very sexy man, even if he did look a tad...gaunt. In spite of the cast on his arm, he moved his body with ease and self-assurance.

"What's wrong?" she asked, seeing his frown.

He pushed the button for the ground floor. "I'm still surprised every time I see myself," he said with a note of self-derision.

"Surprised? Why?"

"I don't look like I think I should look, like I *feel*."

"How do you feel you should look?"

"I...don't know exactly." He shrugged. "I'm not sure I can describe this adequately, but the guy staring back at me in the mirror looks like he ought to be somebody else."

She felt a tickle of amusement. "Somebody else? What do you mean?"

He gestured at his image. "He looks dead, distant, stern, as if he doesn't smile a lot. Certainly not somebody I'd want to be friends with."

She laughed. She didn't know where it came

from; it welled up from some forgotten place. Once, a long time ago, they had laughed a lot.

He gave a deep sigh. "Good, you can laugh. I was beginning to worry about that."

"Oh, why?" His comment took her by surprise.

"You've been looking painfully serious ever since you arrived and that added to the fact that I look like I never crack a smile either made me seriously concerned about the kind of marriage we have. I was having visions of something dreadfully dreary." He glanced back at himself in the mirror with a grimace of comic despair. "I don't *feel* like somebody who never smiles, but look at this face: dead, gloomy, grim. Is that who I really am? I just don't remember it?"

She swallowed uneasily. *Yes,* she wanted to say, *that's how you were in the end; that's why I left you.*

He gave her a tortured look. "Oh, please, don't tell me it's true. I can't remember the slightest thing about who I am and I already can't stand myself."

She laughed again, amazing herself. "No," she said, "I mean, yes, you used to laugh and smile a lot." *Used to.* She needed to choose her words carefully, wisely, so as not to give herself away. It wasn't like her to be worried about every word she uttered. She wasn't used to deception.

Deception—an ugly, dishonorable word. She cringed. There was no other way, not if she wanted to stay here and help him.

"Used to?" he asked. "Before my accident, you mean? Well, good, that's encouraging." He frowned again and jabbed a thumb at his reflection. "How did I end up with this face looking like death warmed over?''

She scrambled for an answer. "Well, you were in a serious accident, you broke your arm, your ribs are bruised, you lost your memory. You...you could have been dead." She shivered. "Surely nothing to warrant hilarity."

"No, I suppose not."

"You *suppose* not?"

"Okay, of course not."

"It's no wonder you look like you went through the wars. And you're not sleeping well with your arm in a cast and your ribs hurting."

"And you weren't with me to give me TLC," he added. He took her hand and squeezed it. "But now you are."

The elevator came to a stop and the doors slid open. "Well, I feel much better already," he commented. "Just knowing we're both able to laugh is a comfort." He held onto her hand as he led her through the lobby and out the front door into the balmy summer evening. It was still light and the air was fragrant with the scent of sun-warmed evergreens. Beyond the woods lay the Pacific Ocean, and here and there Amy caught a glimmer of water in the distance between the trees.

The restaurant came into view around the first bend. Nestled among the towering trees, it had a large wooden deck furnished for outside dining. They settled themselves at one of the small tables set with cheerful tablecloths, candles and flowers and almost instantly a waiter materialized to take their drink orders.

"I'll have a sherry, please, medium dry," she said.

Michael ordered a glass of Chardonnay.

"Sherry," he said when the waiter had departed, "how very European. Interesting."

"That's what I usually have," she said.

"I'm going to have to get to know you all over again. It'll be a...fascinating experience."

"You may not like me," she said, wishing she'd not said it the moment the words flipped out of her mouth.

His golden gaze held warmth and humor. "I already like you. You're my wife. I married you."

She bit her lip. "But you don't remember that."

"True, but I have enough confidence in myself to know that I must have married you because..." he paused fractionally "...because I was passionately in love with you."

Her heart lurched. She stared uneasily at the small flower arrangement on the table.

"Hey," he said softly. "Don't tell me it's not true. Don't tell me I married you because of your money, or because I couldn't get enough of your body, or I won you in a poker game or..."

She managed a shaky smile. "No, no. We got married for all the right reasons."

He heaved a sigh of relief. "Good. Well, then, we have nothing to worry about. I'll just fall in love with you all over again, and I'll try and hurry up."

Nothing to worry about.

How wrong he was.

The waiter came with their drinks, and a moment later another one appeared with their menus.

"Our specialties today..."

Everything he mentioned sounded mouthwatering, but then, after eating reconstituted freeze-dried goop for weeks on end, this was not a surprise.

After the waiter had departed, Michael cocked a questioning brow at her. "You asked for salmon; I thought you said you're a vegetarian."

"I decided seafood doesn't count." She sounded like a nitwit. She couldn't help herself. An old pattern suddenly back: making nonsensical statements, having silly conversations, joking, challenging. Something had pushed an old forgotten button.

His brows arched higher yet. "You decided fish belongs to the plant kingdom?"

"I like seafood."

"That's not an answer to my question."

"Don't push me." She glowered at him. "Okay, I exaggerated. I'm not really a vegetarian."

He puffed out a long breath and grinned. "Oh, boy, I was worried there for a while."

She decided not to pursue the subject. In the scheme of things, it was hardly important. Instead, she asked him about the Aurora and his work and if he liked Oregon.

"I know this sounds awfully egocentric," Michael said after a while of this, "but I wonder if we could talk about me. I'd like to get to know me." He gave her a charming smile. "Just tell me the good stuff, though; the bad stuff can wait until I remember it myself."

The bad stuff. She felt a sudden chill. She put her glass down carefully, focussing on the table.

"All right. Let's see. You like the outdoors, hiking, sailing, all that sort of thing. And you like read-

ing, all kinds of books, and you play the piano.
You're really good.''

''What kind of music?''

''Everything. Classical, jazz, and wild, funny stuff
you make up yourself.'' She went on talking and he
did not interrupt. She became aware suddenly of his
eyes on her, dark and intense. She sipped her sherry.
Her head felt light.

''You're staring at me,'' she said, wondering
what he was thinking.

He reached for her hand. ''I'm trying to figure out
what made me fall in love with you.'' He grimaced
apologetically. ''Sorry, I don't mean it the way that
sounds—as if it would be hard to imagine at all. It's
not.''

''Well, good,'' she said a bit dryly, surprising herself.

''Well, help me out here.'' His warm, brandy-
colored eyes probed hers. His hand played with her
fingers, sending spirals of sensation through her
bloodstream. She wanted to withdraw her hand, but
it didn't seem like a very wifely thing to do. ''Why
don't you tell me what you think?'' she suggested.
''After all, here I am, brand-new all over again, so
to speak.''

Brand-new. The word echoed in her mind. The
green of her eyes would be new to him, the reddish
gold of her hair, the shape of her body.

He would not know what she looked like under
her clothes or what it felt like to touch her and make
love to her.

She did not want to have thoughts of kissing and
loving, but here she was anyway, having them—

how wonderful it had always been—full of passion and laughter and magic.

Until it had stopped. Until they had no longer kissed and touched each other, no longer even wanted to look into each other's eyes, afraid to see what was there. No longer talked. And finally silence had taken over and all the passion and laughter and magic had gone from their lives.

"What I think," he said, "is that I like looking at you, that I'm glad I'm not alone, and that I must be a very lucky man."

The waiter brought their first course. Glad for the distraction, Amy took an eager bite of the smoked salmon pâté.

"Tell me," said Michael, stirring his soup, "how did we meet? Was it love at first sight?"

She bit her lip, feeling the lightness of laughter floating back into her heart like joyous, healing music. Ah, she remembered well and even now, after all these years, it was easy to feel the humor. The first time she'd seen him, she'd screamed bloody murder.

She shook her head. "No, not love at first sight. You fell in love with me just before that. Just before you saw me for the first time."

"I fell in love with you *before* I saw you?"

"Yes." A little devil was stirring inside her and with it came the unexpected urge to tease him. It was the strangest feeling—light and carefree; as if she'd been hypnotized by his charm, the gleam in his eyes.

He swallowed a spoon of soup. "Where did we meet? Where were we?"

"In a hotel bathroom."

He tilted his head and studied her. "This is very interesting."

"Oh, it was." She grinned at him. "It was a very...eh...unusual meeting." She paused. "I was naked."

"Naked?"

"Well, it *was* a bathroom. And I had just stepped out of the shower."

His expression displayed equal amounts of mirth and confusion. "But you said I fell in love with you *before* I saw you."

"I was singing in the shower, and you heard me when you came into the room and you told me you were instantly...enchanted. Your word, not mine. I'll never understand."

"Why? I can certainly understand being enchanted by a woman's voice."

"I can't carry a tune in a bucket, I've been told. I only sing in the shower when no one can hear me. Or at least when I *think* no one can hear me."

Amusement lit up his eyes. "I fell in love with you at first sound, then."

"Yes."

"And next I saw you naked." He leaned back in his chair. "What happened?"

"I screamed."

He grinned. "I mean, how did I get to be in your hotel room? I wasn't a common hotel thief or something, was I? Looking to steal your jewels?"

"Would I have married you?" she asked haughtily.

"Maybe your morals aren't better than mine."

She glared at him and he shrugged innocently. "Well, I don't know, do I?"

"My morals are sterling, thank you."

"Well, then, I'll assume mine are too, your having deigned to marry me and all that." He spooned up some more soup. "So, what was I doing in your room?"

"It was nothing more dramatic than a simple little mistake. They'd given you the wrong key. Your room was across the hall."

"Mmm. And I just marched in and opened the bathroom door when I heard you sing?"

"It was open already. I don't like all that steam collecting on the mirrors and I wasn't expecting strange men to come barging in."

"Okay. So, then you saw me and you screamed. Then what?"

"I lunged for a towel, tripped over a bath mat and fell into your arms."

"You are kidding me." His voice was low and incredulous.

"No." She laughed; she couldn't stop herself. "It was like some awful cheap slapstick movie. You in your fancy suit, holding me, dripping wet with nothing on."

"How lucky can a man be?"

"You were almost arrested, that's how lucky," she said dryly. She took a bite of the luscious pâté and savored it slowly. "Mmm, this is yummy."

"I fell in love with you and you called the *cops* on me?"

"Not exactly. My friend was in the room next to mine and the connecting door was open. She heard me scream, ran in, saw you, called the security people and so on and so forth. Anyway, it really was just a mistake and actually, all in all, it worked out very well." She grinned. "For the rest of my stay the hotel gave me the royal treatment, afraid I'd sue them, I guess, and you sent me flowers and invited me out to dinner."

"And you accepted?"

"Yeah. I was at loose ends that night."

He glowered at her.

"Okay, all right. I liked your hair. You have good hair for a man, nice and thick and just a bit unruly." She'd loved running her fingers through it.

"What else?"

"Your nose. It's crooked."

His hand went up and touched it as if he had to check the truth of it. "It feels like it was broken."

"Somebody socked you one and broke it. It was in high school."

"Mmm. So you accepted my dinner invitation because I have good hair and a crooked nose."

"And you were funny," she added generously. She took the last sip of sherry. She was feeling breezy, carefree. "You made me laugh. You were the funniest, sexiest crooked-nosed man I'd ever met."

Before the evening had ended she'd been hopelessly in love with him—with the sexy sound of his voice, with the devil dancing in his eyes, with all the masculine charm of him that seduced every feminine cell of her.

Six months later they were married and moved to the island.

The day she had fallen naked in his arms had been the day she had arrived in Rome to get ready for the wedding of her best friend, who was marrying a drop-dead gorgeous Italian. Amy was the maid of honor. Michael was an American cousin of the groom.

Spring in Rome. And there was Amy, meeting the man of her dreams. She'd roamed the city with him in a rosy haze of romance. He was wonderful! He was magnificent! Just looking at him gave her delicious thrills. She could easily imagine his picture displayed on the front cover of entertainment magazines, his eyes dancing, his teeth gleaming, his curly hair sexily tousled—the latest Hollywood heart-throb.

Their time together in Rome could not have been more romantic—starry nights, lovely dinners at sidewalk restaurants, holding hands during the beautiful wedding of her best friend.

Now, years later, she told Michael everything, seeing the light in his eyes, noticing the sharp lines of his face soften. She told him about their own wedding, about her parents—the best parents in the world—who now lived in Madrid; about St. Barlow, the wonderful beaches, their circle of eccentric friends. She told him how much she had enjoyed her work as a guide, taking small groups of people on hikes into the rainforest-covered mountains.

Something strange was happening; she was vaguely aware of it on the fringes of her consciousness. As if she were under a spell, a magic spell that allowed her to remember all the joy and fun and happiness and nothing of what happened later. She was in a protective bubble and in it with her was Michael with his laughing face and seductive eyes. And he seemed real, so real.

It did not last.

Reality intruded crudely when two women were seated at a table nearby. They were talking, one in a soothing, calming tone, the other in a loud, hostile one.

"What do you mean, I shouldn't divorce him?" she hissed. "He's not the man I married. He doesn't even *talk* to me anymore! He doesn't *care* about my feelings! Should I live with someone like that for the rest of my life? Are you nuts?"

The words held a bitter familiarity and Amy felt the bubble burst and her happy mood evaporate.

Michael gave her a wry grimace. "I believe I'll skip dessert."

Back in their suite, the door locking out the rest of the world, Michael turned to her with a smile. "That was a wonderful evening," he said. He stood in front of her—close, too close—and her legs began to tremble.

"I want to kiss you," he said.

Her heart skittered and lost its rhythm. She couldn't move, couldn't say anything. She was acutely aware of the longing emanating from him, an intense, seductive energy quivering in the air around them.

"I feel kind of funny about kissing you," he said with a little quirk of his mouth. "As if I shouldn't, because I don't know you. But I really want to, and in a way that makes me feel like I'm a...like I'm just letting my animal instincts take over, but then again you are my wife so..." His voice sounded a little husky. "What the hell," he muttered. He cupped her chin in his right hand and lowered his mouth to hers.

She had no defenses against her own instinctual

response to the familiar feel of his warm mouth. She closed her eyes, yielded to him.

In the last couple of years she'd been kissed by other men—not many, not often. But the frozen core of her had never melted, her senses never truly stirred.

Now, everything was melting, everything was stirring. Her blood sang, her heart danced.

Warning bells rang on the far fringes of awareness. *No*, she thought feebly, *I shouldn't let this happen.* But it was merely a faint murmur.

He drew away and looked at her, his eyes dark and smoldering. She knew that look.

He didn't know her, recognize her, but he wanted her. The desire was there in his face, his body, as clear as it had been in his kiss. She stood very still, her blood throbbing.

She saw him withdraw, felt his hand slip away. He turned his back and crossed to the window, stared out into the night-shrouded forest.

"I'll get my memory back, you know," he said on a low note. "I've decided I will; I'm just sort of accepting it as a given and that makes me feel more positive about the situation. Brooding and worrying about it are not going to be productive, that much I know." He turned to face her. "I am glad you're here to give me moral support, even if I don't know you."

She winced, she couldn't help it, and he was instantly repentant.

"I'm sorry," he said quietly. "I don't mean to hurt you. More than anything else, I wish I could remember my feelings for you as my wife. I should be able to tell you that I love you and that I missed you when you were away and I should be carrying you off to bed and making passionate love to you, but I can't even do that with this blasted cast on and my ribs aching and..." He groaned. "I feel like a fool saying these things to you."

"It's all right," she said huskily, not daring to meet his gaze, struggling with her own longing. She felt like a fraud. She *was* a fraud.

"They're there, you know," he said softly. "My feelings for you are all still there—they're just in hiding right now. And it will be wonderful when they're back."

"How do you know?" she whispered.

He grinned. "All I have to do is look at you, and I know. I feel it."

He was so wrong, so desperately wrong. She stared down at her hands, clasping them to keep them from trembling. He touched her bent head, a quick, tender caress.

"It'll be all right, Amy," he said softly.

No, she wanted to say. *It won't be all right, Michael. It can never be all right again.*

The next morning was punctuated with nerves and unease. She helped him with his clothes again and made them a simple breakfast in the small kitchen. Then he kissed her briefly on the cheek, as he had done hundreds of times before, and left for work. Simple things that nonetheless stressed her nerves.

Amy poured herself another cup of coffee and contemplated what to do next. It was a glorious summer day and she was free to do as she pleased. She had the keys to a rental car, which was parked outside, and keys to the house, which was on the far end of the hotel grounds, a nice walk through the woods, Michael had said.

She didn't want to see the house. It was his house, not hers, and she didn't want to know where he would be living after she had gone back to Philadelphia.

Stop it, stop it, a voice ordered her. *Go see the place. Just do it.*

It was a dream house. Perched on the wooded cliffs, it offered a panoramic view of the ocean and the rocky mountains jutting out into the water on the left. Built of weathered cedar and field stone, it lay nestled in the trees as if it belonged there, part of nature. Amy wandered through the spacious rooms, admiring the floor-to-ceiling windows with their breathtaking view, checked out the large modern kitchen and felt a painful twinge of...what? She wasn't sure what the feeling was.

She took the car and explored the surroundings, scouted out the small coastal town, and had a bowl of clam chowder for lunch at a seaside restaurant.

It was almost four when she came back to the apartment, finding a beautiful flower arrangement on the coffee table. She picked up the little card, seeing Michael's own familiar handwriting. He'd selected the flowers himself. *"To my wife,"* the note read. *"I'm glad you're here. Love, Michael."*

Love, Michael. The simplest words in the world and they made her throat close up and her eyes burn with tears. She reread the note several times, then put the card down, just as she heard the door lock click and saw Michael entering the room.

"You're here," he said, sounding pleased. He brushed his lips across hers in greeting.

"Thank you for the flowers," she said awkwardly. "They're beautiful." She picked up the card and fingered it nervously.

"Last night was the best night I've had since I woke up in the hospital," he said quietly. "I was happy being with you, in spite of the fact that I don't really..." He stopped himself.

"...know me to be your wife," she finished for him.

He met her gaze, his eyes warm. "I *do* know you to be a woman I'm very attracted to." He gave her a teasing smile. "I find that very encouraging, don't you?"

Her breath caught in her throat. She couldn't let this happen. She should have thought this out much more before coming here. She nodded and bent her head. "Yes," she said, feeling like a liar. She fingered one of the roses. "It's just...it all seems so...strange."

He didn't reply, and when she glanced up a moment later, she saw him watching her, a quizzical expression on his face. He lowered himself in one of the deep, comfortable chairs and reached out his hand to her. "Come here," he said softly. Blindly she moved forward and he drew her onto his knees, put his right arm around her, holding her close. She tensed, fighting for control. Their faces were so close and there was no way to avoid it.

"Why are you so nervous?" he asked. "You're all tense."

"I don't know what to feel," she said miserably.

He laughed. "I'm your husband. You love me because of my hair and my crooked nose."

"But you don't know me, and that makes it all

so unreal." *And you're not really my husband,* she added silently. *And I shouldn't be sitting here on your lap with your arm around me.*

"I may not know you the way you are used to my knowing you, but all day I thought about you and about what you had told me about our life together. All day I was looking forward to coming to the suite and finding you here. To know my *wife* was there and I could kiss her hello when I came back. It makes me feel like a very rich man."

She wanted to die right there in his arms, or sink away into a hole in the ground and never come out. She kept her head bent, afraid to look at him, afraid he would see the deceit in her eyes.

"For two weeks after I came to in the hospital I didn't know I had a wife. I didn't know I had a sister. I didn't even know myself. I lay there thinking I was alone in the world. I had this intense feeling of isolation, of not belonging. And now, here you are, my wife, someone I share my life with." He lowered his face and she felt his mouth against her cheek. "And I'm very glad," he added softly.

She sat very still, hardly breathing, wishing she could accept his words, the meaning behind them. She yearned with a sudden fierce pain for his tenderness, his passion, his love, the way she had once known it—in another time, another life.

"Look at me, Amy," he said.

She lifted her face to his, and she wondered if he could see the longing in her eyes, if he could feel the trembling of her body against him.

"Michael," she whispered, "I—"

His mouth closed over hers and the years fell away. All the pain and sorrow instantly dissolved in the magic of his kiss. Her heart and body were hungry, and he drew from her an instinctual response. She let it happen. Kissed him back with all the need surging through her. She felt the warm, familiar intimacy of his body against hers and dizzy desire spiraled through her.

On the fringes of her consciousness she knew a sense of wonder—how easy it was, how natural…

Finally, breathless, he eased his mouth away from hers, resting his cheek against hers, saying nothing.

She breathed in consciously, slowly. His arm was still around her and she did not want to move, to open her eyes. She wanted to savor this magical sense of intimacy between them. It felt so good, so right.

"Mmm," he whispered, "that felt very familiar."

"Yes," she said softly.

"We must have done this before." His voice was light with humor.

"Once or twice," she said, matching his tone, marveling how easy it was. "When we had nothing better to do." She lifted her cheek away from his and smiled into his eyes.

He chuckled. "I'm beginning to have really good feelings about this marriage of ours. When my memory comes back, it will be like opening Christmas presents—all sorts of wonderful memories and surprises."

She felt as if she'd fallen into icy water. *Oh, Michael,* she wanted to say, *it won't be like Christmas.* It was too late to hide her face. His expression sobered a little as he observed her.

"Amy, don't look so stricken," he said soothingly. "It will happen. I *know* it will."

There was something not right and he couldn't put his finger on it. Michael stood in front of his bedroom window, unable to sleep, thinking of Amy. Thinking again of the kiss, and how her whole body had yielded to him so naturally, and her mouth had seemed so hungry for his. Yet, in every other way, Amy was nervous and strangely reticent for a loving wife. Almost as if she wasn't comfortable with him, as if...

Well, of course she wasn't comfortable with him. He was acting like a stranger, treating her like a stranger. She kept staring at him, studying him, as if she didn't really recognize him anymore.

Was he no longer the man he used to be? Had the accident, losing his memory, somehow changed his personality? It was a terrifying thought. Yet he sensed something similar when he looked at his face in the mirror, seeing something...wrong.

CHAPTER THREE

AMY wandered through the house and looked at the furniture she knew so well, the neatly labeled cardboard boxes, the rolled and wrapped rugs. She glanced at Michael, seeing his unsmiling, serious face. She felt the tension emanating from him as he surveyed the room to see if anything was familiar in the jumble of tables and chairs and boxes the movers had delivered that morning. She'd called him at the office as soon as they'd finished unloading and he'd come right over.

She saw his face light up as he noticed the piano. He stood in front of it in two quick strides, not bothering to find the stool, and let his right hand fly over the keys, tapping out a fast rhythmic tune, cheery and lively. Then he turned to her and grinned. "You're right, I play the piano."

"And you're very good, too," she said lightly, relieved to see his grin. "Just wait till you can use both hands." He was good at everything he did, everything he tried. *Except being a husband,* came the unbidden thought. She pushed it aside.

He wandered away and she watched him surveying the room.

"Now this is what I call a chair," he said, plunking himself down in an oversized, overstuffed chair, contemporary in design and infinitely comfortable.

Her heart turned over. He'd zeroed in on the chair as if by instinct. There was suddenly an odd, unfocussed look on his face. He held out his hand. "Come here," he said huskily.

She moved toward him, knowing she couldn't do anything else. He took her hand, drew her closer.

"We used to sit in this chair together, didn't we?" he asked, searching her face for affirmation.

She nodded. The love-nest chair, they had called it. They'd used to sit in it, arms around each other, kissing, fondling. The chair would hug them like a snug nest.

And she'd sat in it alone, when he was not home, crying for hours and hours.

He drew her onto his knees, his right arm around her. "This feels so right," he said.

"You remember," she whispered.

"Yes. I remember sitting with you in this chair." His voice was unsteady, but there was a light in his eyes. "It's vague, not...very visual, but I feel it, I know it. It's...real." He kissed the corner of her mouth. "I don't want to go back to the office," he whispered against her lips. "I want to sit here with you and keep remembering."

Fear gripped her. "Do you see anything else?" Images, memories and photos she had not looked at in years flashed through her mind. *Let him remember other things,* she prayed, *but not this, not yet.*

"No," he said, his cheek against hers. "The more I try, the more it escapes me. I guess I have to take it the way it comes." His voice held a mixture of disappointment and resignation.

"It hasn't been so long, Michael," she said.

"I know. I suppose this is the time for me to cultivate the virtue of patience." His tone had lightened. He eased her away from him. "And now I'd better get back to the office and get ready for my meeting.''

She slid off his knees, and watched him come to his feet and straighten his tie. Then he kissed her quickly and strode out the door, and she was alone in the house, alone with the trappings of her past.

Two years ago, when she'd left Michael, she'd taken with her only some personal things, clothes, the photo albums, a few books. Two suitcases was all she had taken with her from her life, her marriage.

She'd wanted to leave everything behind, to never see it again, and here it was again, haunting her, following her—her whole married life all wrapped up in pale green paper and cardboard boxes.

And she had to unwrap it all piece by piece, bring it back into the light, bring it back into her sight and consciousness. There was something terribly cruel about it all.

She sat down on the edge of the sofa, trembling. She thought of what any of these boxes might contain, things she even now could not bear to see, to touch, to smell. *I can't do this,* she thought.

She got up and started wandering around again and opened windows everywhere. She needed air to breathe.

The kitchen. She could start with that. The cooking things would be safe enough.

She took a break at one and ate the sandwich she'd made that morning. She sat on the porch, savoring the pungent scent of firs and pines. Back in the house, she emptied the boxes for the dining room and the living room. Artwork, knick knacks, decorative cushions, the bright rugs.

Michael called halfway during the afternoon. "Does it look like home yet?" he asked.

She laughed, amused at his eagerness. "It looks like a tornado hit the place. All these empty boxes and there's a mountain of wrapping paper. It will take me a few days before I get all this put away properly."

"Of course. I know. I'm just...I guess I'm ready to feel settled a little."

She felt a rush of compassion. "I know."

Does it look like home yet?

Home. A place to belong, a place to be yourself, to feel comfortable, a place to share with your loved ones. Of course that was what he wanted, needed.

"Don't get yourself too tired," he was saying. "I have something special planned for tonight, dinner included."

"Okay," she said obediently, smiling in spite of herself. "What is it? What are we doing?"

"It's a surprise."

She laughed, recognizing the old Michael talking. "And you're not going to tell me, right?"

"Right."

She gave a long-suffering sigh. "Okay, okay."

After she'd hung up she glanced around. Master bedroom. Safe enough? She took a deep breath and slit the boxes open and began taking out the contents. Michael's clothes, shoes, pictures, bedding. Nothing of hers was there, nothing of the personal things she had left behind. What had he done with them? Given them away? Thrown them away? Not that it mattered.

She arranged everything in the closets and drawers, dreading to be finished, to have to do the other boxes.

Bedroom two or three? Her hands shook. She was terrified. She couldn't do it. She hugged herself, swallowing miserably, and the phone rang.

She fled into the living room, picked up the receiver and managed a flat little hello.

"Amy? Is that you? It's Melissa. I got your new number from the office." She sounded uncharacteristically nervous. "Are you moving into the house?"

"Yes." Amy rubbed her forehead. "The movers delivered the shipment this morning. I'm in the middle of unpacking it all."

"Oh, is this a bad time to talk?"

"No, no, it's fine." *Anything but unpacking those boxes*, she thought. She sat down on the floor, her back against the wall. "How are you, Melissa?"

Once Melissa had been her sister-in-law and close friend; now it felt awkward talking to her. The years of separation and all that had happened gaped between them.

"Fine but bored stiff." A slight pause. "Amy?" she said then, hesitation in her voice.

"Yes?"

"How's everything with Michael? I didn't want to call you right away, but I'm so worried."

Amy took in a slow, deep breath. "It's strange. He really doesn't know me, Melissa."

"Oh, Amy," she said disconsolately, "I'd so hoped for a miracle. That…you know, that when he saw you again, his memory would just pop right back. You were his *wife*. How can he not recognize you?"

"I don't know, Melissa." Amy shifted the phone to her other ear. "I want to ask you a question."

"Sure, anything."

"When you talked to Michael, before you even thought of trying to find me, why didn't you tell him about us? About..." She closed her eyes and swallowed. "About what happened."

"Oh, Amy, I just couldn't make myself," Melissa wailed. "He had so much to deal with all at the same time. I just didn't want to load him down with...with it before he could even remember the good things, the happy times. It just didn't seem fair, somehow, especially not over the phone, and...and I already had to tell them about Mom and Dad..." Her voice trailed away.

Michael and Melissa's parents had died in a plane crash and Amy imagined it had not been easy for Melissa to go over this part of their history with him.

"Well, yes, I guess you're right." Amy stretched her legs out in front of her and stared unseeingly at her bare toes. Melissa had tried to protect Michael; she could hardly blame her.

"I know I did a terrible thing to you, asking you to go to him without him even knowing the truth," Melissa blurted out. "Are you angry with me? I wouldn't blame you, you know."

"I'm not angry with you. To be honest, I don't know what I'm feeling half the time. It's all so confusing."

"I miss you, you know," Melissa said on a sigh. "You just disappeared and I felt terrible. You were like the sister I never had."

Amy felt a stab of guilt and regret. "I know, Melissa, I'm sorry."

A short silence on the line. "Were you in Philadelphia all this time?" Melissa asked.

"Yes."

"Have you been…all right? I mean…" She couldn't finish the sentence.

"All right? I suppose so." What was all right?

"Did you…?" Melissa hesitated. "Is there someone else? Are you seeing somebody?"

A man, she meant. Amy gave a humorless little laugh. "No, there's no man in my life. I'm not interested."

"Michael hasn't as much as looked at another woman since…since you left."

"Melissa…"

"I know, I'm totally out of line, but I want you to know."

"Melissa, what happened between us wasn't just a little squabble that…that…" Her voice died away. She didn't want to discuss this.

"I didn't mean that! I'm sorry, really."

How strained the conversation was, nothing at all like the talks they used to have, sharing laughter and unself-conscious confidences. She knew Melissa felt it too, it was obvious from the tone of her voice.

"I'd better let you get back to your work," Melissa was saying. "Please promise me you'll let me know if Michael remembers things again, anything."

"Of course, I will, Melissa. He'll probably call you himself."

Amy was glad the conversation had come to an end. Then she remembered what she had been doing and her stomach tightened. She couldn't get herself up from the floor. Pulling up her knees, she wrapped her arms around her legs. She was tired, so tired.

She heard the front door open. Michael. Michael to the rescue. The other boxes would have to wait till tomorrow.

Relieved, she scrambled to her feet and ran her hands through her hair. She hadn't known how late it was. He strode through the door, looking immaculate and sophisticated in his business clothes, and quite out of place in the disorganized room.

"There you are." He dropped a kiss on her cheek. "You've been busy." His gaze swept around the living room. "This is very nice," he said. "I like that rug, very colorful."

He was looking around like a visitor, like someone who had never seen any of the things in the room. He wandered quickly through the rest of the house, coming back in the living room where she was sitting on her knees on the floor, bundling sheets of paper. She glanced up at him, and he smiled, but the dull bronze of his eyes gave him away.

"Patience, remember?" she said gently.

"Yeah, builds character." His tone was dry. He reached his right hand out to her. "Come on, you've done enough for now. Let's get back to the hotel and relax for a while."

She took his hand and let him help her to her feet.

"Are you all right?" she asked, knowing the answer already.

One corner of his mouth twisted upward. "Of course I'm all right."

He did not let go of her hand as they walked back to the hotel.

Back in the room Michael tossed his jacket on a

chair, pulled off his tie and poured them each a glass of wine. "How would you like to go to the beach, have a picnic dinner and watch the sun set?" he asked. "Just the two of us."

Amy took a sip of the wine. A picnic dinner at the beach. It was the kind of thing they'd used to do on the island. She fought against the images flooding her mind.

"Unless you'd rather eat in a restaurant?" he asked.

She did not have the courage to disappoint him. She shook her head. "No, the beach will be nice."

"I thought you might like it. You've been cooped up inside all day and…eh…it sort of occurred to me." He frowned a little. "We…you said we liked being outside, outdoors."

"Yes, we do. I'd love to breathe some fresh air for a while." It was just like him to think of this. The old, generous, loving Michael wanting to make her happy.

She showered and slipped into comfortable white cotton pants, a soft green T-shirt and sandals, tying a sweatshirt around her waist in case it cooled later on.

Michael had managed to change into jeans and a shirt, which she quickly buttoned for him. It was not a long walk to the beach and the evening air was summery warm. She loved the smell of the ocean and the feel of the breeze on her face.

The restaurant had packed them a picnic meal and Michael carried the hamper and Amy the Mexican blanket to sit on. They settled themselves on the colorful rug, their backs against the rocks, and Amy peered into the basket with curiosity. Wedges of a cheese tart with roasted red bell peppers, basil, and olives. Tabbouleh and fresh pitta bread. Grapes and peaches. Even a bottle of wine and two glasses were part of the spread.

"Mmm...this looks scrumptious," she said. "I didn't realize how hungry I was."

"Then dig in," he said succinctly.

She dug in.

It was delicious.

"I love watching you eat," he said with a grin.

"You do? Why?"

"You do it with such passion."

Passion. Good heavens. She chuckled. "Well, food is good. Good food, anyway. And we need to eat, so why not enjoy it?"

"You don't have to convince me." He scooped up some more tabbouleh.

He was eating with quite an appetite himself, she noticed. Maybe if he kept it up he'd lose some of the gauntness in his face.

He put down his wine glass and captured her left hand. "Look at that," he said, glancing over at the horizon.

The sun was low, streaking the sky and clouds with flames of color reflected in the sea.

Amy sighed with awe. "That's gorgeous." She watched the brilliant display, aware of his fingers playing with her hand. "We had beautiful sunsets on the island," she said quietly. "We'd sit on the veranda when you came home from work and watch them."

"Seems like a nice way to finish a working day," he answered.

"Yes, it was." She began to eat the grapes, feel-

ing him playing with her fingers—touching, stroking, as if rediscovering every little bone, the shape
of her nails, the texture of her skin. He stroked the
palm of her hand with his thumb, a feeling so erotic
a flush of warmth heated her skin. She tossed the
rest of the grapes back in their container, slipping
her hand out of his.

"Another glass of wine?" he asked, spindrift-
cool.

She shook her head. "One's enough." She let
herself fall backward onto the blanket and stared up
at the dusky sky. Here and there the pale glimmer
of a star was beginning to show.

"If I fall asleep, wake me up when the tide comes
in," she said, and closed her eyes. The words had
come almost automatically and she regretted them
the moment they'd left her mouth. This was not her
speaking; this was the old Amy, teasing, tempting,
inviting.

The old Amy. The old Michael.

She could not allow herself to get trapped in a
time warp illusion. She scooted upright before
Michael could reply.

"Just a joke," she said, making herself smile.

Leaning lazily back against the rock, he studied
her with a devilish glint in his eyes. She had the
uncanny feeling he knew exactly that her words
weren't meant to be taken seriously, at least not had
they been spoken by the Amy from the old days.

"Let me guess," he said slowly, seductively, "do
we like making love outside?"

It was suddenly hard to breathe. "Yes," she said.
What else could she say?

"Places like the beach?"

"Yes." She wanted to change the subject. She reached for another grape and popped it in her mouth. "Mmm, these are sweet."

"Hey," he said softly, "am I embarrassing you?"

"No. Why would I be embarrassed?"

"I have no idea." She caught the odd little note in his voice. He reached for her hand again and tugged at it. "Lie down, put your head in my lap," he said softly.

She didn't know how to refuse. *Don't think, don't feel, just do it.* She shifted a little and put her head in his lap as she had done countless times before. She stared up into the sky, feeling tense and nervous.

He stroked her hair, slowly, sensuously, and she began to relax. Such a wonderful feeling, she thought languorously, aware suddenly how much she had missed being touched in the last two years.

"Tell me," he said, "where else outside do we like to make love besides the beach?"

"Other places." *Please,* she prayed, *I don't want to talk about it.*

You have to, a little voice told her. *You have to tell him everything.*

Not everything.

His hand trailed down her cheek. "Be more specific. I want to know."

She swallowed and kept staring at the sky. It was incredible, unreal, that he did no longer know this, no longer had any recollection of making love with her outside in those idyllic hideaways they had discovered on their exploration of the island.

She braced herself. "On the island there was a place in the forest in the mountains," she began, "near a little brook. The water was very clear and cold." She could still see it in her mind and tried her best to describe it to make it real to him.

As she talked, she could feel his gaze on her, felt his hand feathering along her cheek, her jawbone, her chin.

She moistened her lips. "And there was another place we liked to go, on the other side of the island, the Atlantic side. The coast is very rough there with rocky outcroppings and tidal pools. We'd go climbing and hiking there, and one day we found this perfect little cave overlooking the ocean."

He was silent, perhaps trying to make a mental picture of what she had described. His hand feathered across her throat, lower and lower, as her heart beat faster and faster. His hand touched her breast, lightly resting there, and warmth suffused her.

In the cave their lovemaking had always been passionate, wild and urgent like the ocean, primal like nature around them. She took in a slow, calming breath. The air was full of the sound of the ocean, the waves breaking. It would be so easy now to believe they were there again in that small cave—the lost fairy tale found again, resurrected as if in some magical time warp. It would be so easy to reach out and make love to him now.

But this was another ocean, another time, and the fantasy could not last. She should not allow herself to be seduced by an illusion, because that was all this was.

So, a little voice said, *who cares? Enjoy it while it lasts. What's wrong with a little happiness?*

He slipped his hand under her T-shirt, resting for a moment on her bare stomach.

"The two of us in a cave," he said in a low voice. "I'm trying to imagine it."

The sound of the sea pounded in her ears, or was it the throbbing of her heart? She lay very still, feeling his warm hand move higher, move the strap of her bra down and lift her breast out of the cup. He held it in his warm hand, rubbing her nipple with his thumb, and heat surged through her body.

She had not made love with any man since Michael, had not felt any desire. Now, it was as if a fire was ignited in her, its flames licking at her every cell, her senses acutely aware of every sound and scent and touch.

"I want to make love to you," he said, his voice low and full of hunger.

"I thought...with your cast and your ribs..."

"I don't give a damn about the cast, or my ribs," he said roughly. "I need you, I need to be close to you. I need to know what it feels like to make love to my *wife*." There was a husky, tormented note in his voice. "Amy...don't you want me?"

The waves crashed against the rocks, exploding into bursts of white spume shimmering white in the moonlight. Over and over. The sound filled her mind, washed away thought.

"I want you," she whispered. She ached. Her body pulsed with need and she felt lost in the sensations, unwilling to fight them.

"Then what's keeping us?"

"I...I don't know."

"I don't either." He paused. "Sit up," he said softly. "Put your legs here."

She straddled his thighs and he curved his right hand behind her head and reached for her mouth like a drowning man, kissing her with a passion that left her weak and trembling.

Breathing raggedly, he eased her away from him a little and with his right hand he began to tug at her shirt. "We've got too many clothes on," he said, his voice unsteady.

Together they got rid of her T-shirt and bra. He rested his face against her breasts. "You feel so good," he murmured.

Her breath was coming in shallow little puffs. She leaned into him, wanting more closeness, more skin to touch, but too much of their clothes were still in the way. She felt his mouth, hot and moist, taking in one nipple, then the other, and desire spun wildly through her blood.

She fumbled with the buttons of his shirt, her awkward, eager hands finally managing to loosen them. She eased the left sleeve over his cast first, then freed his other arm. She tossed the shirt aside.

She rested her hands gently on his chest, the hair tickling her fingers. "Does it hurt?"

"No," he said huskily. He leaned back against the rock, his eyes closed, his breathing shallow.

Under her palms she felt the thumping of his heart—strong, comforting. It was a miracle he was alive, a miracle his heart was beating—a miracle that had brought her here to feel it again.

He could have been dead.

Dead.

For a moment a terrifying blackness swirled through her. It set off a convulsive trembling and a painful little sound struggled out from deep inside her.

Don't think. Don't feel. She took in a deep breath,

trying to relax, but instead tears welled up and rolled soundlessly down her cheeks.

"Amy? My God, what's wrong?"

She couldn't speak. She wrapped both her arms around his neck and pressed her cheek against his.

"You're crying," he said. "Amy—"

"I could feel your heart," she said shakily.

"I've got one," he said dryly.

"You're alive," she whispered.

He chuckled. "I was, yes, a minute ago."

She made a strangled little sound, half-laugh, half-sob. "I'm sorry," she said thickly. "It just overwhelmed me, I guess. I don't know what happened. It just...I don't know."

She did know, but she could not tell him. His right arm held her close, his hand stroking her bare back, soothing her. She couldn't stand this, she couldn't bear the strain of all those mixed up feelings, the need to love him the way it had been, the way it could never be again.

"I wish you knew me," she whispered. *I wish you knew me the way it was when everything was happy between us,* she added silently.

"Yes," he said, and she heard the longing in his voice.

I'm not being fair to him, she thought miserably. *I'm not being fair to myself. I don't know what to do.*

They sat for a while, silently, not moving. Finally his arm fell away from her back. "We'd better get back," he said calmly.

"I'm sorry," she said again.

"Don't apologize, Amy, please," he said gently. She came to her feet and pulled on her T-shirt, not bothering with her bra, which she stuffed in her bag. Then she helped Michael with his shirt, avoiding meeting his eyes.

"I didn't mean to spoil this," she said, the words nearly sticking in her throat.

"It's all right, Amy."

But it wasn't all right. She chewed her lip, feeling helpless.

In silence they gathered up their things and made their way back to the apartment.

Michael stared at the file on the desk in front of him and realized that he had no idea what he'd been reading. All he could think of was Amy, his wife.

His present conscious mind had known her for all of two days and he wanted her with a passion that stunned him. There had to be something else there, something under the surface—some emotional manifestation of all the forgotten memories of love and desire. How else could he possibly feel so strongly?

He closed the file and came restlessly to his feet. He stood in front of his office window and stared at the wide expanse of sea and sky, seeing only Amy's face as she had looked at him the night before at the beach. He wanted to make love to her, he yearned to know her again as he must have before, feel the intimacy and the belonging. She was his wife. It was all right to feel this way, to want her, to love her. It was a *good* thing.

Still, he felt like a fraud. He could not offer her the husband he had once been, the lover he had once been. He could only offer her what he was now, what he felt now, and he wasn't sure it was good enough, real enough. He wasn't sure it wasn't just plain, physical lust.

Not that there was necessarily anything wrong with plain, physical lust; in a healthy marriage he assumed it could be a source of great fun and delight.

He closed his eyes with a frustrated groan. He saw in his mind her clear green eyes, her soft mouth, the dewy texture of her skin. He loved her. He *knew* he did.

But he did not want to make love to her with her thinking that it was just lust. He should take it easy, until—

The ringing of the phone on his desk broke off his thoughts. He turned away from the window and pushed the speaker-phone button.

"Yes?" He sat down and rubbed his neck, trying to clear his mind.

"Mr. DeLaurence," his secretary said, "Ms. Jennifer Casey is here to see you. She says you know her."

Michael grimaced. That was an easy thing to say these days. "Send her in, please." The name meant nothing to him.

The door opened and a slim woman in an elegant business suit entered. Curly chestnut hair framed an open, attractive face and she stared at him with wide brown eyes. He did not know this woman.

"Michael?" Apprehension trembled in her voice.

He stood up and she came rushing forward and threw her arms around his neck. "Oh, Michael, I'm so sorry about what happened to you!"

CHAPTER FOUR

FOR a moment Michael simply stood there not sure what to do, aware of the faint flowery scent of the woman's perfume. Then he withdrew from her gently.

"Please, sit down," he said, feeling frustrated by his inability to recognize her and not knowing how to respond to her. Was she a good friend he should have kissed on the cheek? A long-lost cousin?

She didn't move, just looked at him, searching his face. Then she slowly turned and lowered herself into a chair, looking defeated. Instead of taking the chair across from her, Michael retreated to the one behind his desk, feeling the need for distance.

"Oh, Michael," she said softly, "I can't believe this. I don't know what to say."

"I suppose you could start by telling me about yourself," he said, hearing the faintly wry note of his own voice.

Nervously, she moistened her lips with her tongue and tucked her hair behind her ears. "This is so weird, Michael." She drew in a deep breath and made an obvious effort to pull herself together. "All right, then. We met on St. Barlow several months ago, while I was doing a consulting job for the hospital, computer network integration. My company is based in Seattle."

She had a melodious, sing song voice, beautiful

expressive eyes. He did not want to notice this, yet he did.

"It was a big job," she went on, "and there were problems so I came back several times and I was staying at your hotel. We got to know each other well, Michael." She gave him a pleading look, as if begging him to remember. "We spent a lot of time together." She bit her lip. "You don't remember anything?"

He shook his head, feeling trepidation slithering through him.

"It was all rather complicated because you were moving to Oregon and my job takes me here and there and everywhere, but we were going to try and work it out so we could see each other whenever possible. " She paused and he could feel the loud, panicked beating of his heart.

"We have something special, Michael. You…we are…" Her voice trailed away.

"I'm sorry," he said, feeling his stomach twisting. *Something special?* What were they talking about here? Was he crazy? Amy's face flashed before his eyes and all he wanted at that moment was to get the woman out of his office, fast.

"What are we going to do, Michael?" she said, her voice soft and fearful.

"About what?"

"About us."

His chest tightened. He was trying to stay calm, to absorb what she had told him, to understand the ramifications. "Under the circumstances, I think we should do nothing," he said.

"You don't need to let me off the hook,

Michael," she said, giving him a faint smile. "I don't scare away easy."

This wasn't what he wanted to hear. "I need to put my life back together again and it might take a long time." He tried to sound businesslike, yet doing it made him feel unkind. He didn't want to see the hurt in the woman's eyes. What had he ever said to her? Promised her?

"I wish I knew how to help you," she said ruefully

"There's nothing you can do."

She studied him for a silent moment. "You seem like a stranger, Michael," she said sadly.

"I feel like a stranger," he returned, and managed a little smile. "Even to myself."

She made a helpless gesture with her right hand. "The plan was for you to fly to Seattle to see me in two weeks," she said quietly. "I take it you don't want to come then?"

His mouth went dry. He had a wife. What was he doing with this woman in his life?

"Yes, it's better."

She looked at him for a long, silent moment. "Michael, you can't push me away this easily." She came to her feet. "I'm not ready to give up on our relationship, but maybe it's best if you give yourself some time under the circumstances. It must all be very traumatic for you."

"Confusing and frustrating at least," he acknowledged, and came to his feet as well. "I appreciate your understanding, Jennifer."

She met his eyes. "Promise me something, please. If you change your mind, call me, okay?"

He nodded and went to open the door for her. "I will."

"Goodbye, Michael. Take care of yourself." She kissed him briefly on the mouth. "I'll be in touch."

Please don't, he wanted to say, but didn't. He felt sick. What had he done? What kind of man was he?

It was early afternoon when Amy saw Michael striding up to the front door. She hadn't expected him until later.

"Hi," she said, as he entered the room. "You don't look happy."

"I have to go to Los Angeles for a couple of days," he said flatly. "Business. Somebody wants to do a movie and use the Aurora for the setting." He dragged his hands impatiently through his hair. "I didn't want to have to leave you alone so soon; you just got here."

"When do you have to leave?"

"I'm taking the next flight out."

"And this came up just suddenly?"

"No, no. Connor was supposed to go, but his wife went into labor this morning, a month early, and that leaves me. Believe me, this is not what I want right now, but I have no choice."

"It's all right. Work is work." She sounded perfectly agreeable.

He frowned. "Yes, and my marriage is my marriage and I just found out I had one." He studied her for a moment. "Would you like to come with me? Can you be ready in an hour?"

Los Angeles. Under normal circumstances, she would have loved to go, but it occurred to her that if he were gone, she'd have a little breathing space. She needed distance, physical and emotional.

"If it's business, you'll be busy most of the time, won't you?" she asked, making her tone casual. "Why don't I stay here and get the house in order? Then, when you get back, we can move in." It sounded perfectly reasonable, she hoped.

"If you prefer." Was there disappointment in his eyes? She wasn't sure, but she felt guilty anyway.

After he had left, Amy let out a sigh of relief. She needed to be alone like a parched desert traveler needed water.

Last night they had almost made love, and she had wanted it more than she'd ever wanted anything. But what she had wanted was not real, had only been an illusion.

It had been a mistake to come; she should have thought about it more thoroughly, but in fact she had not thought about it at all. She had just done it. What lunacy had possessed her?

And now she could barely bear the strain. She felt guilty about the deceit. Guilty every time she saw the longing and desire in his face, knowing he would never find what he was searching for. And she was scared of her own yearnings when memories seduced her and the past came rushing back and all she wanted was to hold onto it, own it again.

She could leave. She could leave before Michael came back from LA.

The thought stopped her short, gave her a sudden sense of overwhelming relief.

Nobody was forcing her to stay.

If she worked quickly, she could get the house

ready for him, then write him a long letter explaining everything—that she was no longer his wife, that he no longer loved her, that in truth he didn't want her at all.

She turned away from the window before thinking further, before she'd stop herself. There was much to do.

For the rest of the day she worked frantically, trying to keep her mind occupied with practical matters. In a couple of days it would all be over and she'd be safely back in Philadelphia.

Michael called from Los Angeles at night. "Just wanted to hear your voice," he said. "I'm hardly gone and I already miss you."

She wanted to sink into the ground.

"I keep thinking about you and I'm having a hard time concentrating on my meetings," he went on. "I wonder what's wrong with me?"

Oh, please, she didn't want to hear this. She felt mean and unworthy. With a strength she didn't know she possessed she rallied a separate part of her brain, the cool, calm, unemotional part. She straightened her back.

"Probably just a virus," she said lightly, almost frightened by her own acting skills. "Take a couple of aspirin and drink lots of fluids."

He chuckled. "I don't think that's going to cure what ails me," he said slowly. "As a matter of fact, I think it's quite incurable."

She squelched all emotion, but the effort made her legs tremble. "That might be a problem, because if you can't concentrate on your work, you're going to be without a job and then what?"

"You're a big help," he said.

"Anytime." She sank into a chair, feeling boneless.

"How are you doing?"

"I'm fine. Unpacked lots of stuff."

"I don't want you to work too hard and exhaust yourself," he said.

"I climb mountains and don't exhaust myself," she said dryly.

"Right, I forgot. I keep seeing you as this short, slim, sexy woman with huge green eyes who looks like she'll break in two if I blow at her."

Amy groaned. "Oh, please, Michael."

He laughed. "I have to go. They're waiting for me. I'll see you soon."

"Bye," she said, replacing the phone. She sat in the chair for several minutes, trying not to dislike herself too much. It didn't work.

So what was wrong with her? She was going to do what was best for both of them.

Michael jerked upright in bed, heart pounding, his body damp with perspiration. An overwhelming despair had dragged him out of sleep and for a moment he simply sat there, sucking in air, trying to calm down.

He switched on the bedside lamp and glanced around. He was in a hotel room, generic, clean, impersonal. He was in Los Angeles, not in an empty house on the island. He'd been dreaming, that was all.

Amy was in Oregon, at the Aurora, asleep in her room. He glanced at the phone next to the bed. He wanted to hear her voice, to know she was there. It was too late. He'd wake her. He switched off the lamp, lay back down and closed his eyes, which was a mistake.

In his mind he saw again the pale blue note he'd seen in his dream, saw the handwritten words as clearly as if he were looking at them in reality. Fear swirled through him. There was a horrible sense of clarity about the images in his head.

But it was nonsense, of course. Just a dream plaguing him, feeding on his irrational fears. He sat up again, turned on the light and picked up the book he'd been reading. Then, unbidden, another image flashed though his mind. A woman's face. Glossy chestnut hair, big brown eyes.

Jennifer Casey.

His stomach clenched painfully and he tossed the book across the room in a burst of anger. Or was it something else? Fear? Guilt?

He did not want to think about Jennifer Casey, nor remember the hurt he had seen in her eyes.

Amy slept restlessly and when daylight finally began to filter into the room she was relieved.

After a cup of coffee and some toast she went straight to the house and went to work. She was confident she'd be able to finish up today, and tomorrow morning she'd pack her things and leave. Michael was coming back later that day, he'd said, around dinnertime. It was best to be practical about it.

As she worked, she tried to compose the letter in her head, but she couldn't make herself put the words together. After all this time, the memory of what had happened was still intolerable.

The phone rang. Her pulse skittered. *Don't let it be Michael,* she prayed silently.

It was Michael.

"Good morning," he said. "How's my wife?"

She closed her eyes. "I'm fine. Busy."

"Too busy to talk to me?"

"No." It was the only answer she could give. She forced herself into her acting mode. "And what about you? How is your work going?"

"It's going, but you keep interfering."

"*I* keep interfering?"

"You keep insinuating yourself into my thoughts. You have taken up permanent residence there. And I like it."

"Well, as long as you keep some mind-space for work-related thoughts."

"It's a struggle," he said dryly. "My thoughts about you are so much more interesting."

She didn't want to hear this, knew where it would lead if only she'd play along. She remembered similar conversations, long ago, when Michael had been away from home on trips. They'd sit in bed and talk on the phone—teasing, thrilling, intimate conversations she'd hoped nobody was intercepting because she'd have been mortified.

"I hope nobody can hear you," she said now. "Where are you?"

"I've said absolutely nothing indiscreet," he stated. "Not that I don't want to, mind you. I have definite urges in that direction—make amorous, suggestive propositions to my wife over the phone. Is that something new or did I do that before?"

She sucked in air. "It's not new," she said.

He chuckled. "Good, I like that about myself. I want you to tell me all about it when I get back."

She wouldn't be there when he got back. She steeled herself. "You didn't say where you're calling from. Somebody's private office?"

He laughed. "From a public phone, and someone with green hair and a ring through his nose is hovering so I should do the polite thing and let him—maybe it's a her—have a shot at it."

The conversation over, Amy dropped her head on the kitchen table and tried to calm herself enough to get to her feet and find a pen and writing pad.

Half an hour later she still sat at the kitchen table, staring at a blank piece of paper, the pen idle in her hand. She couldn't find the right words. They weren't there; they simply did not exist.

She saw Michael as he was now, strong and courageous, a man able to laugh in the face of his problems. A man who wanted to know her and love her as his wife, convinced his feelings for her would come back, and who was half in love with her already. How could you tell a man like Michael, who was struggling to get his life back, that all those feelings were useless because they had no foundation in reality, that they were only based on illusion and deception? She would strip him of all that he was holding onto now, all that he thought was good in his life.

She thought of the flowers he'd given her. *To my wife, I'm glad you're here.* She thought of what he had said: *It makes me feel like a very rich man. I keep thinking about you.* She felt an overwhelming rush of emotion.

She couldn't tell him.

And she couldn't leave him. It would be a terrible thing to do to him now. It would be unconscionable to desert him when he needed her.

The only thing she could do was finish what she had started. Be with him and help him until the amnesia would clear up and he would learn the truth. And then go on from there, deal with the consequences, no matter how difficult it would be.

And somehow she would have to resist falling in love with him all over again, because this warm, funny, sexy man wasn't really Michael at all.

It was a Michael who no longer existed.

And she couldn't leave him. It would be a terrible
thing to do to him now. It would be unconscionable
to desert him when he was so hurt.

The only thing she could do was finish what she
had started. The only thing she could do was carry
on, would wake up and he would learn the truth.
Maybe someday she would have to tell him.

CHAPTER FIVE

WORKING almost automatically, Amy got the rest of
the furniture arranged, boxes emptied, the beds
made up.

To her relief she discovered nothing else disturbing in any of the boxes. What she had been afraid
of finding was gone. She felt a sudden hard knot of
pain in her chest. What had Michael done with all
those things?

Had he thrown them all away? Given them away?

He hadn't cared. All he wanted was to forget
about what had happened, to just go on and pretend
nothing was wrong.

She sat on the floor in the room designated as a
home office sorting through bins of supplies and remembered the last painful months they'd lived together on the island. The old, familiar anguish filled
her again and she tasted the bitterness of it in her
mouth.

Michael had hidden in his office, coming home
later and later, exhausted. She had tried desperately
to talk to him, to no avail. Her tears made him ir-
ritable and impatient. He drowned himself in work,
staying away more and more.

In contrast, she had been unable to work, to take
out happy hikers and show them the marvels of the
mountains. She'd spent hours staring into space,
hours crying, hours sleeping, drugged by pills the
doctor had prescribed her.

70

The emotional distance between them grew larger and more silent every day, and her anguish more acute. She would look at his closed face, seeing no longer the man she loved, but a stranger who did not want to be with her.

Amy stared blindly at the files in her hand. In the end she had thought she had hated him and the feeling was so agonizing she could no longer bear being with him, feeling the silence suffocating her. All she had wanted was to get away from everything, to start over without him.

And now she was back with him, but he was no longer that silent, angry stranger she had left. He was again the man she had loved so long ago, the man who enjoyed her company and made her laugh. The man who made her blood sing and her senses dance.

And she wanted this man back with all her heart and soul.

But how could she have what did not really exist?

Michael felt a rush of warmth as he heard Amy's voice on the other end of the line. It was his third call of the day and he felt like a love-sick teenager.

"I should have persuaded you to come with me," he told her ruefully.

"Why?"

"Because you wouldn't be alone." What he should have said, he knew, was, *I don't want to be alone.*

"I can handle it, Michael," she said, amusement in her voice.

"I'm not sure *I* can," he returned, adding a note of mock drama to his voice. "I'm a bit new at this husband business and I worry. I don't like thinking of you being alone—helpless, defenseless, without my protection.''

She gave a choked little laugh.

"Anything could happen," he asserted.

"Like what?"

"You could wander off and get lost in the woods," he improvised. "You could be kidnapped by aliens."

He heard her chuckle. "Yes, you're right. I hadn't thought of that. But you would rescue me, Michael; I'm not worried."

"True. I would." He grinned at nothing in particular. Just talking to her made him feel good. He could sit here and listen to her happily for the next two hours.

"I've got almost everything done," she was saying, her voice breezy. "All that's left is a stack of boxes of books. I'll leave them for another time. There's no hurry."

"We can do them together some time."

"Yes, that would be nice."

"I can see it already," he said, "a cozy fire, romantic music on the CD player, and you and I sorting books, sipping a little wine, maybe reading to each other."

Images suddenly danced in his mind. The two of them on a big bed, reading to each other, Amy laughing. An open window with a night sky visible and a breeze billowing the curtains. Amy in a short white nightgown, slim legs crossed yogi style, long shiny hair flowing freely around her face and shoulders.

He held his breath and lightness filled him.

"Amy? Is that something we do? Read to each other?"

He heard her catch her breath. "Yes. Do you remember that?"

"It was just...a little flash, a sort of vision. I could see us do it. Tell me, what sort of things do we read. Poetry?"

"Not usually." She gave a soft little laugh. "Our reading sessions are not very high-minded affairs. We read humor pieces, harried travel tales."

"The *Kama Sutra*? In bed?" He could not resist.

"Are you on a public phone?" A note of censure in her voice.

"Definitely not," he said, with feigned indignation. "I'm in my hotel room, alone and lonely."

"Nobody's entertaining you?"

"Well, yes, but not for another ten minutes. Drinks, dinner, the works with a bunch of film people. I wish you were here and I'd skip it all." He found his wife infinitely more exciting.

"I'm flattered."

"I mean it. I could read to you from the *Kama Sutra*."

"Do you happen to have that handy?" she asked dryly.

"No, but I could get it." The mammoth bookstore across the street from the hotel probably carried it in several languages. "Amy?"

"Yes?"

His teasing mood dissolved. He closed his eyes. "I can't wait to see you again, to be home with you."

He was aware of the briefest of pauses. "Tomorrow," she said then, her voice a little unsteady. It

was all she said. As he replaced the receiver, he felt
a twinge of apprehension.

Amy blew out a slow breath as she hung up the
phone. She should have said something more, she
knew, something about looking forward to seeing
him too, but the right words hadn't come.

Having finished work for the day, she went back
to the hotel suite and fixed herself a quick sandwich.
Then she packed her belongings and moved them
over to the guest room in the house. She stacked the
photo albums on the coffee table. The package
wrapped in white trembled in her hand and without
further thinking she quickly hid it in a drawer in her
bedroom. Later, later.

She had a shower, wrapped a long robe around
her and settled herself on the sofa to watch a movie
on TV, a comedy she hoped would relax her before
going to bed.

Michael searched the suite at the Aurora, rushing
from room to room, fighting panic. She wasn't there.
Her clothes were gone, her bedroom and bathroom
empty.

On impulse he had come back tonight rather than
tomorrow evening. After his phone call with Amy,
all he wanted was to come home. He'd packed his
bag, made his excuses to the film people and caught
a taxi to the airport. The dream he'd had the night
before had unsettled him. He wasn't one to take
much stock in dreams, but this one had hit a bit too
close to home for comfort: Coming home and finding her gone, a note on the table saying she'd left

him because he wasn't the man she remembered and she didn't love him anymore.

And here he was in the midst of the nightmare again. No sign of Amy anywhere and it was past midnight. He should not have gone to LA by himself. He should not have left her alone. He gulped in air and searched around wildly for a note.

There was no note to be found anywhere.

He took a deep breath and forced himself to calm down. This was ridiculous. He should get a hold of himself. Why would she want to leave him?

Because you're not the man you once were. Because to her you don't seem to be her husband any longer.

He closed his eyes. *Because she found out you were having an affair before the accident.*

No, he couldn't believe it, could not afford to believe it. It was all a sick joke. He pushed the thought away.

There was a simple explanation, such as that she wasn't here because she'd moved into the house already. It was as simple as that.

Like a man possessed he ran through the woods to the house, and when he saw a faint light shimmering through the trees he felt almost dizzy with relief.

He entered the house quietly, finding her asleep on the sofa in the living room, dressed in a soft green robe, the TV on. For a few minutes he just stood there, drinking in the sight of her, resisting the urge to haul her into his arms and kiss her senseless.

She was lying there so peacefully, a faint smile curving her mouth as if she were dreaming of something happy. The long robe had fallen away from one of her legs—a shapely leg, bare and lightly tanned. Her toenails were polished a luscious, berry-pink he could almost taste on his tongue. She lay on her back, one arm thrown over her head, and the soft curve of the top of her breast peeked out above the robe. The reddish gold of her hair gleamed in the lamplight like rich honey. His gaze lingered on her face, her cheeks flushed a peachy pink with sleep. He took in the freckles on her nose, the full lips, slightly parted. She looked soft and vulnerable and young. He felt himself fill up with love and sweetness and a deep hungering. She was his wife, and he was the luckiest man on earth. And even though things were difficult right now, everything would be all right in the end. He had to believe that; it was the only thing that kept him going. She was the link to his past, the love in his life.

He sat on his haunches in front of the sofa and gently touched her hand. He did not want to frighten her.

"Amy?" he whispered.

She stirred. Her hand moved under his and held onto his grasp.

"Amy, it's me, Michael. I'm home."

She moaned softly and her eyes opened to give him a dazed, unfocused look. "Michael?" she muttered.

"Yes, I'm back."

"Oh." She sighed and her lids drifted closed again. "I'm glad," she murmured, still half asleep. Her hand slipped out of his grasp. He reached up and stroked her head, her hair like silk under his hand. He cursed his inability to simply lift her up into his arms and carry her to bed, his bed…to have her close all night, to feel her warmth. He refused to think further.

The sofa was big and comfortable; she'd be fine there for the night. He came to his feet and went in search of a blanket and a pillow. The bed in the master bedroom was made up and men's clothing hung in the big wardrobe—his, he presumed. There were no women's clothes. He found them in another bedroom, but not very many, which seemed a little strange. Maybe she hadn't unpacked them all? The bed was made up and toiletries were set out in the adjoining bathroom. A damp towel hung over the rack. Clearly she intended to sleep in a room of her own. He grimaced, well, that was what he had suggested himself when she'd arrived, hadn't he?

Gathering up a pillow and blanket, he traced his way back to the living room. Amy hadn't moved an inch. He covered her up and she opened her eyes again, smiling sleepily at him.

"Lift up your head," he said softly. "I have a pillow for you."

"Okay," she said obediently, and managed to lift her head enough for him to slide the pillow under it.

"Michael?" she murmured sleepily.

"Yes."

"Kiss me."

He kissed her softly. She gave a low moan and reached her arms around his neck.

"More," she murmured.

He kissed her again, deeper, longer, his blood suddenly pounding through his body. Semiconscious, she was all soft, yielding desire, wanting him.

And he wanted her. How he wanted her, this woman he didn't know.

He loosened her arms from around his neck as gently as he could and retreated to his room, amazing himself. He was a saint. He gave a frustrated groan. He was an idiot.

Amy awoke to birdsong and sunlight. She was lying on the sofa, she realized; she must have fallen asleep watching the movie. But the television was off and someone had covered her up and slipped a pillow under her head.

She was suddenly wide awake. She jerked upright. Somebody was stirring around somewhere in the house and she smelled coffee.

Michael?

She'd been dreaming about him last night, holding him, kissing him, wanting him. After that she didn't remember.

He came into the room as if she had called him, carrying a small tray with two cups of coffee in his right hand. He was wearing a loose pair of athletic shorts and his hair curled damply around his head. Her pulse leaped. He looked so good, his broad chest bare, his body strong and tanned. Not even the miserable cast on his arm took away from the fact that he was all healthy, vibrant, unself-conscious male. She'd seen him like this a thousand times, sailing and swimming, and still she could not help thinking how much she enjoyed looking at him.

"Well, good morning," he said. "I thought you'd never wake up."

"You're back," she said unnecessarily.

"Unless you're just dreaming me." He gave her a lopsided grin.

She shook her head. "No, I'm not."

She *had* been dreaming, she remembered. About kissing Michael, about feeling really happy...

He deposited the small tray on the table in front of her. A drop of water glistened in his chest hair and she smelled soap and aftershave. She took the cup of coffee he handed her, wishing she wasn't so instantly, intimately aware of him, wishing he had more clothes on, even just a robe. But belting a robe was a struggle and it was easier just to pull on some shorts, she knew. She took a careful sip of the coffee, trying not to feel the erratic beat of her pulse.

He sat down next to her on the sofa. "I came back last night. Don't you remember?"

She shook her head. "No."

"You gave me a warm welcome."

She frowned. "I did?"

"Yes, you did. You kissed me. Warmly, passionately, I should say." There was no mistaking the humor in his voice

The dream. Maybe she hadn't dreamed kissing him at all, maybe it had actually happened. She rubbed her cheeks. "I thought I'd dreamed it," she said.

He laughed softly. "No. And it's all right you know. I'm your husband; you can kiss me any time."

She concentrated on sipping the hot coffee. "I thought you'd be back this evening."

"I didn't want to stay away any longer." She caught the odd note in his voice. Glancing up from her coffee, she met his gaze.

"Why?"

"I wanted to be with you. I had a frightening dream about you." She saw the sudden darkness cloud his face, felt apprehension slither along her nerves

"What...about?"

He hesitated. "What was so terrifying," he said slowly, "was that it seemed so real. Mostly my dreams seem to be nonsense, but this..." He frowned. "I dreamed that I came home and you were gone. You'd left me, just like that. And you wrote a note saying I wasn't the man you married and you didn't love me anymore."

It felt as if a big hand pressed down on her chest. It had happened, two years ago, and yesterday she'd thought of leaving him again. And he had dreamed it, known it, remembered it on some intuitive level. And it had frightened him—this strong, competent man who was never afraid. It had frightened him enough to come back home ahead of schedule.

But she hadn't left. She swallowed, feeling a wave of relief.

"I'm here," she said softly.

"Yes. Yes, you are." He looked into her eyes, and she felt a rush of warmth, felt his hungering like her own. He put his cup on the table, took hers out of her hand and set it down as well.

For a brief moment she sensed his hesitation, then he leaned toward her and kissed her, a deep kiss that made her blood rush wildly through her veins. He gave a soft moan low in his throat. "I don't know what I would have done if you had been gone," he muttered. "I need you, Amy, I need you so."

"I need to know what it feels like to make love

to my wife," he had said that night on the beach. She knew with a sudden, aching clarity what had been hidden by those words, what was hidden by the words he had just spoken. He wanted, needed more, so much more than just a physical loving. He wanted to know her as his wife; he wanted himself back, he wanted his life back.

And then another thought flashed through her head as his mouth ravished hers, as his hand opened her robe and curved around her breast. *I want you back, too. Oh, Michael, I want you back.*

She responded to his kisses with a hunger that was frightening until suddenly he gently withdrew from her, taking her hand in his.

"Amy…"

"Make love to me," she whispered, "please, please."

"I want to, but…it's…" He paused, giving a frustrated groan.

"What?"

"I feel like a fraud, somehow." There was anguish in his voice. "I'm a fake masquerading as your husband. It isn't fair to you."

"Not fair?" she asked softly.

"Because you want to make love to your husband and I…don't feel like I'm your husband because I don't know…don't remember what it feels like."

She glimpsed in his eyes the terrible, lonely emptiness he normally hid so well. Her heart contracted. "You're not a fraud, Michael," she said. "You lost your memory; that doesn't make you a fraud."

"I can't give you my real self, Amy."

"I want who you are now," she said, hearing the little catch in her throat, knowing the truth of what she'd said. *I want who you are now because you're the man I fell in love with.*

He regarded her with shadowed eyes. "Is it enough?"

She nodded. "Yes, oh, yes." And suddenly she found herself smiling. She laid her cheek against his. "Because I love you, Michael."

The words had come without conscious design, had come from a deeply hidden part of her—the old Amy surfacing again, loving him, wanting him, knowing it was right and good.

She felt a convulsive tremor go through his body, felt his right arm tighten around her. "Amy," he said in a strangled voice. "Oh, Amy..."

And then there were no more words, just their mouths and hands and limbs—just a hungry, turbulent kissing and touching, until, breathless, they drew apart a little and gazed dizzily at each other.

Her robe had fallen open, the belt come loose. He reached out and gently slipped the robe off her shoulders. "I want to see you," he said softly, "all of you."

She stood up and the robe fell to the floor, pooling at her feet. Standing there naked in front of him, she felt oddly shy, aware that in his conscious mind he was seeing her for the first time.

The first time. The hotel bathroom. Coming out of the shower, dripping wet. Michael in his expensive suit, watching her.

It's okay, she told herself.

Michael came to his feet as well, and got rid of his shorts, and he stood in front of her in the bright morning sunshine, all male and aroused, his face full of desire and love.

A new day. A new promise. A sweet thought drifting through her mind.

He reached out and stroked her cheek. "Are you going to scream this time?" he asked, and the humor in his voice told her he knew what she had been thinking about a moment earlier.

She moved her body closer, leaning into him, aching to feel him against her. "No. I don't need any rescuing."

"What do you need?" he asked on a low note, trailing his fingers gently along her chin and throat, down to her right breast, cupping it and stroking the nipple with his thumb. Sparks of desire danced through her body.

"You," she said on a breath of air, her legs feeling weak. "I just need you." How true it was—she needed him as she had needed him always, this man who stirred her heart and soul and body. She was having trouble breathing, trouble standing on her feet.

She saw his expression, felt the air around them charged with emotion and passion. He put his right arm around her and drew her intimately against him. She felt the heat of him, felt her nipples aching against his chest.

"Oh, Amy," he groaned, and the naked need in his voice clutched at her heart. Love, desire and a mishmash of emotions suffused her and she didn't resist, simply allowed the mysterious energy of the moment to carry her with it.

They lowered themselves back onto the sofa, limbs and bodies trembling, clinging to each other.

"I want to love you so much," he murmured in

her ear. "I want to make you happy. I want to make you feel I'm..."

"Shh," she whispered. "You will, Michael. You already do. It feels so wonderful to hold you like this." Her body sang. "And I want to make you happy too," she added softly. She found his mouth, kissed him deeply as she moved her hands over him, discovering, marveling, doing what she had always loved doing, giving him pleasure with her mouth and hands and body.

He loved her back, made every cell of her spring to life as no one else could ever do. In this magic place devoid of thought and time, he was no stranger to her body. She felt lush and vibrant and whole.

They brought each other to the limits of endurance, and a wild, primal urgency took over. She felt him inside of her, a fullness so complete and deep she cried out softly. Agonizing pleasure...holding on, holding on.

There was no holding on—no controls, no boundaries, no moorings, only a giving up and a glorious freefalling through a pure and blissful space.

They clung together wordlessly, sated, and their bodies stilled into languor. Amy wanted nothing more than for the moment to last, to preserve the deep joy of fulfillment like a precious gift.

"Amy?" His voice was low and soft, barely registering. She wondered how long they had been sitting there, the morning sun washing over them.

She opened her eyes, meeting his regard. She smiled at him. The birds were chirping in the trees in the garden, a lovely, joyous sound. What time was it? She had no idea.

"I love you," he said, his voice spilling over with tenderness. "Do you mind if I say this?"

Because I've only known you a few days, she heard him think as clearly as if he'd spoken the words.

Tears sprang to her eyes and she shook her head. "No. No, of course not," she said tremulously, brushing her mouth against his. Did he think she'd not find his words believable? She believed him, needed to believe him.

"Don't cry," he said against her lips. "You worry me when you cry."

She offered him a quivering smile. "I'm just happy."

"And that's why you cry? Am I supposed to understand that?"

"No. It's a woman thing. Don't even try."

He laughed softly. "All right. As long as you're happy."

"I'm happy." She kissed him again. "Happy, happy, happy."

He laughed. "Will you still be happy if I tell you our coffee is cold?"

She chuckled and slipped off his lap. "I can fix that."

She brewed fresh coffee and concocted eggs ranchero for breakfast. After he had left for work, she put on a CD with Strauss waltzes and danced around the house, twirling around by herself on bare feet, joy making her light as a feather. Finally she collapsed in a chair, breathless, grinning at herself. She was a fool. Fortunately, nobody could see her here— no close neighbors peeking through the windows, no nosy housekeeper yet.

She spent the rest of the day doing ordinary, mundane chores, but time went by as if she were dreaming, as if nothing could touch her, as if nothing existed in her thoughts but Michael and the way he had loved her and the way he had made her feel. *I love you*, he had said. She hugged the words to her like a priceless treasure.

She cooked them a delicious dinner and afterward they leafed through the photo albums, studying the collection of images that made up their life together—their wedding, their house on the island, their friends, the beaches and the forests. They laughed about a snapshot a friend had taken of Amy pushing Michael off a dock into the bay. They found a picture of Amy hugging a sappy-looking baby goat.

Amy grinned. "This was taken at Sasha's goat farm. Remember I told you about her? She started her own business raising dairy goats and making goat cheese. She sells it all over the Caribbean to fancy resort hotels and restaurants. The baby goats are so cute."

More photos, more stories. They laughed and teased each other—touching, kissing, until the tension was a live thing between them.

They made love again that night and again the day after that and all the days that followed that week, as if they had been parched and starved for each other and could never get enough. He slept in the big bed with her, and she did not care when he was restless in the night. She'd reach for him, half awake, wanting him, loving him.

They went on long walks in the mountains, leisurely drives along the majestic coastal road. They attended parties and were invited to dinner. She'd never been happier.

It was like being hypnotized, like being caught in a witch's spell in an enchanting fairy tale. She wanted it to last. She wanted his loving, his caring his laughter. She wanted the past back.

She blocked out everything that had come after that tragic day their life had changed. When whisperings of reason and fear would steal into her thoughts, another voice, another part of her would answer.

He thinks he loves you. Let it be. Let him love you, like he loved you before. Pretend it's real. Forget everything that happened and love him back, like you used to. What is wrong with giving each other happiness?

Because it isn't real, warned the voice of reason. *Because it cannot last. One day he'll know you deceived him.*

She wanted to silence that nasty, rational little voice, wanted not to hear it. She wanted Michael to love her. She needed him to love her.

Even if it wouldn't last.

Michael was in his office, reading his e-mail, finding a message from a certain Matt, a name he knew from Amy's stories. *"We just came back from vacation and heard on the island coconut telegraph about your accident,"* he read. Aware of Michael's amnesia, the man introduced himself as a friend, a doctor who ran the island hospital, married to Sasha, the goat cheese lady.

He had heard from several other people on the

island in the past few weeks—friends by all accounts, yet strangers to him now.

Michael read the message again, feeling an odd
uneasiness he could not identify. It was a perfectly
straightforward letter, imparting island news that
might be of interest to him, offering some medical
information, and giving encouragement. Still, something about the letter disturbed him.

He shook his head impatiently. He was getting
paranoid. How could he have suspicions about
something he didn't even remember? He'd lost his
memory; the last thing he needed was to lose his
mind.

CHAPTER SIX

ON THE appointed day, Michael's cast came off. They celebrated with champagne. Michael wrapped both arms around her and held her tight against him. "This is what I've been waiting to do," he said, "to hold you properly." He smiled into her eyes. "I love you, Amy."

Warmth suffused her and a lump formed in her throat. "I'm glad." Her voice was unsteady.

"It's real," he said softly. "I don't need my memory back to know it."

A flash of fear.

She willed it away. *Live only in the moment.*

"I love you too," she said.

"What kind of affair is this, anyway?" Michael asked the next evening as they were getting ready to go to a party. "I never saw the invitation. Do I have to wear a jacket and tie or can I just go like this?"

He was wearing jeans and a polo shirt and looked at her hopefully.

"It's not a beach party, Michael. You're going to have to do better than jeans." Not that he didn't look great in jeans, she thought, looking at him. He always looked good.

"Every female with a pulse thinks he's drop-dead gorgeous," someone had told her a few days ago, a woman at the gym. She'd sung Michael's praises

and told Amy she wanted one "just like him," as if he were a piece of merchandise she could pick off the shelf in a shopping emporium.

"I want people to like me for who I am," he said theatrically, "not judge me by the clothes I wear."

"A very worthy sentiment," she said blandly.

"I'm actually contemplating letting my hair grow and having a ponytail," he went on. "All this sitting around in a barber's chair every few weeks is a waste of time."

He was egging her on. She laughed as she slipped into a blue-green party dress. "You'd look very sexy with a ponytail, especially wearing your business suits. But what would you do with all that extra time you'd have on your hands?"

He gave her a devilish grin. "I'd spend it on carnal pursuits."

Michael did not have a roving eye, had never given her any cause for worry or jealousy when they'd been together. He'd teased her about the masseuse and the secretary who'd helped him with his clothes before she'd arrived, but both of them had turned out to be helpful grandmothers with no designs on him.

"Carnal pursuits such as what?" she asked, squinting in the mirror as she put in her earrings.

"Ravishing you." He wrapped his arms around her and nibbled her left earlobe.

"Oh, goody," she said, laughing, and slipped away from him to find her shoes.

According to Melissa, Michael hadn't as much as looked at another woman since she had left him. But of course Melissa hadn't been around to watch him every minute. Had there been other women? Amy wondered. The fact was that before the accident Michael had known he was single.

Proof of this arrived later at the party in the form of a beautiful woman. She was tall as a model, had long black hair, bedroom eyes, and a dress to kill for. Amy felt an instant surge of dislike.

"Michael!" the woman called out in pleased surprise. She approached him with a flirty smile and one hand outstretched, the other clutching a drink. Taking hold of Michael's free hand, she offered him an exaggerated look of concern.

"Michael," she said throatily, "I just got back from Europe and I heard about your accident. I'm *so* sorry, I..." She looked at him helplessly. "You don't know who I am, do you?"

"I'm afraid not," Michael said soberly.

Amy's stomach churned. Little scenes like this had played themselves out almost every day, but this woman made all her antennae shoot up instinctively.

"I'm Julia Morrison," the woman said. "I met with you about—"

"...the advertising campaign," Michael finished. "Yes, I read your name in the files." He smiled politely and briefly shook her hand. "Allow me to introduce you to my wife," he went on. "Julia, this is Amy. Amy, Julia Morrison."

There was no mistaking the shocked surprise in the woman's dark eyes. Then something else flashed across her expression, not at all pleasant, and Amy knew the woman was not happy with the unexpected news of the existence of a wife in Michael's life.

She did not like this woman. She liked nothing about her—not her face, her gorgeous hair, her sexy dress. Not even her damned designer shoes.

Who was she? Michael didn't know, but that didn't mean he couldn't have had a torrid love affair with her before the accident. A *fast and furious* torrid love affair, she reminded herself; he'd only been in Oregon a week before the car crash.

Amy wasn't sure what came over her, but suddenly she felt herself get into gear. Looking Julia straight in the eyes, she faked a bright and confident expression and extended her hand. "Nice to meet you, Julia." How gracious she sounded; she amazed herself.

Julia apparently did not return the sentiment, because she said nothing as they coolly shook hands. Julia turned to Michael and gave him a wide-eyed, innocent look. "You didn't tell me you were *married*," she said huskily. It was clear to Amy that this information was meant as a little poisonous arrow for her.

Michael arched his brows. "Really?" His tone was cool. "Well, I'm afraid I do not recall."

Mercifully, this miserable little exchange was interrupted by a waiter passing edible doodads on a tray. Before he had moved on with his offerings, two other people joined them and Amy caught Julia moving in on her next prey.

Unfortunately it wasn't the last Amy saw of her. They found themselves facing each other again in the ladies' room half an hour later. Amy felt every cell of her body rally to the challenge. This woman was not going to get to her, she vowed. She was going to be in control if it killed her.

"You should watch that husband of yours," Julia said nastily, fluffing up her hair.

"Really?" Amy said, cucumber cool.

Julia looked down at her with undisguised hauteur. "Really," she returned, her voice dripping condescension.

Ignoring the woman's tone, Amy peered in the mirror and applied her lipstick. "So, you too, huh?" she asked conversationally. She rubbed her lips together and examined them.

"Me too *what*?" demanded Julia, eyes narrowed.

Amy shrugged. "Had an affair with my husband when I was out of town," she elaborated, as if Julia were one of an army of females regularly seduced by Michael. She dropped her lipstick back in her bag and offered Julia a pitying look. "You actually *fell* for him?" *You poor naive thing,* her tone implied.

Julia's eyes widened and she seemed stunned for a moment, then she visibly collected herself. "Hell, no," she spat out. "I'm not that stupid! We had lunch once and I saw right through him."

"Well, good for you." Amy swung around and sailed out the door.

Once out of the ladies' room, Amy felt her legs begin to tremble dangerously. Good heavens, what had gotten into her? She could not believe she had said what she had said, insinuated what she'd insinuated. She leaned her back against the wall for support and anchored her feet to the floor.

Then, as she calmed herself, the humor of the situation suddenly struck her and a bubble of laughter rose to her throat.

In search of Amy, Michael saw her coming out of the ladies' room and lean against the wall. For a moment he thought she wasn't feeling well, then he realized he was wrong.

She was laughing. Softly, to herself. He set his empty glass on a side table and strolled up to her.

"So, what's so funny?" he asked.

She looked up in surprise, then she grinned.

"Julia," she said, waving at the ladies' room. "She got nasty mad at me because I'm your wife. She has the hots for you, excuse my language."

He wasn't pleased with this news. He didn't like this Julia and again felt frustrated by his lack of memory, not knowing what he had or had not said to this woman. Why had she been under the impression that he hadn't been married?

"Well, she's out of luck." he said evenly, "she's not my type."

Amy glowered at him. "And if she were?"

He saw her face, knew she was not serious, knew that, in fact, this wife of his trusted him completely and wasn't worried at all. He thought of Jennifer Casey and felt a sharp stab of guilt. Then he pushed the thought out of his mind. He couldn't deal with what he didn't remember. He could only deal with the present and what he knew now.

He managed a smile, draped an arm around her shoulders and drew her close against his side. "Only one woman is my type, and that's you."

There wasn't enough to do in the house to fill her days, so, like a real woman, she went shopping. Usually she went alone, but one day she was out with Kristin, whom she'd met at the gym, and who, after three babies, still had a flat stomach.

"So what are you looking for?" Kristin wanted

to know as they riffled through the racks in a classy little boutique.

"I need things to wear to go out to parties and dinners. Something…nice, fashionable."

"Nice, fashionable," Kristin repeated, apparently not impressed. "How about something feminine and sexy?"

"That too," said Amy. *Why not?*

"Red is sexy," said Kristin, holding out a cloud of shimmering crimson silk "but I'm not sure you can wear it with your coloring."

"No red," said Amy. "And nothing frilly. I'm not a bows and frills person."

"Mmm," said Kristin, tilting her head and studying Amy. "I think what you want is something quietly elegant or simply sophisticated, or maybe… knock-'em-dead sexy."

"All of the above, now that you mention it," said Amy, feeling reckless.

An hour later she'd tried on fifteen dresses, found two she liked and was trying on one more on Kristin's insistence. It was a slip of a thing Amy wouldn't have given a second look because it was all black and way too revealing.

"Black washes me out," she protested.

"There isn't enough of it to do that. Wear lipstick. Just try it. You can't tell by looking at it on a hanger."

"All right, all right."

She shimmied into the thing and stared at herself in the mirror in the fitting room, feeling her breath catch for a moment. The dress was deceptively simple and stunningly sexy. It was sleeveless and short, and the black silk hugged her in all the right places.

Narrow shoulder straps held up a lacy, V-neck bodice that looked as if it belonged in the bedroom. A row of small buttons teased its way down the front, begging to be opened. A dress made for seduction.

She twirled in front of the mirror. It had been so long ago that she had worn anything like this—so long ago since she had *felt* like wearing a dress like this. She felt feminine again—alive, sexy, desirable.

She stood still, staring at herself in the mirror.

Something magical had happened to her—to her body, her feelings, her soul. She could see it in herself, see the glow in her face, feel the tingling of life energy in her blood.

Love. That was what it was.

"Amy?" came Kristin's voice. "Let me see. How does it look?"

Amy stepped out of the little dressing room. "It fits," she said.

Kristin stared at her. "Oh my, yes, it fits. It's gorgeous. It's *perfect*!"

"It's not a tad too…eh, *daring*?"

Kristin grinned and batted her lashes. "Not if you're a Real Woman."

Amy bought it.

Half an hour later she was home again, slipped into the dress once more and inspected her reflection in the bedroom mirror. She could only come up with one conclusion: she would never have the courage to wear this dress in public. Although it covered everything that should be covered, it was too suggestive. She'd never considered herself particularly prudish, but there were limits.

This dress was past the limit and she was an idiot

for having wasted all that money on it. Why had she bought it?

Because she wanted it, that was why. It made her feel absolutely, deliciously sexy. And there was one person to whom she wouldn't mind showing herself wearing it.

She picked up the phone and called Michael. "What are you doing?" she asked. "Something interesting?"

"Reading a very long business proposal," he said dryly.

"Sounds dreadfully boring."

"Unfortunately this one is."

"Well, maybe it will get better," she said soothingly.

"I doubt it. But I shall hang in there and survive."

She grinned. He didn't know what she knew. Having produced some more comforting wifely noises, she said goodbye and hung up the phone.

She pulled on a sober blazer over the dress to hide some of its more come-hither qualities and made her way to the office.

"I need to speak to my husband," she told the secretary. "Something unexpected came up and we...have some serious things to discuss. Would you mind holding his calls?" It was difficult trying to look suitably serious.

Mrs. Applegate, blue hair and all, was a pro. She picked up the phone. "Mr. DeLaurence, your wife is here. She asked me to hold your calls. Perhaps, with your permission, I'll go for lunch now."

Tossing her jacket onto a chair, Amy sashayed into Michael's office, closed the door and leaned back against it. He was sitting behind his desk, looking very much in command in his dark suit, white shirt and tie. Very...respectable. Something needed to be done about that, definitely.

"Hi," she said sunnily. Her hand was behind her back on the doorknob. She reached for the key and turned it.

He studied her with mild surprise, brows raised in question. She'd not come to his office before without his expecting her. She'd certainly never locked the door before. "Hi," he returned, his gaze skimming over the dress. "To what do I owe this pleasure?"

She advanced into the large room. "You sounded as if you needed a little lifting of the spirit," she said, and sat down on the edge of his desk, crossing her legs, like a true *femme fatale*.

He pushed himself back in the chair and regarded her with humor. "An excellent idea."

She swung her foot, dangling her shoe on her toes. "Of course," she said, lowering her eyelids demurely, "I don't want to disturb you." Ah, the thrill of seduction!

He chuckled. "You came here for the express purpose of disturbing me," he stated.

She lifted her head slightly and peered at him through her lashes. "Is it working?"

"Mmm...we'll see. Is that a new dress?"

"Yes." She fingered the top little button of the bodice. "I bought it this morning and I wanted to show it to you. Do you like it?" She worked the little button loose while gazing at him innocently.

His eyes gleamed darkly. "It's a rather... dangerous little piece."

She slipped off the desk, and with a seductive swing of her hips eased around the corner and nestled herself on Michael's lap. "Dangerous?" she asked, trailing her finger along the length of his tie.

"Yes." He put a hand on her bare thigh, exposed by the short skirt. "It might corrupt the soul of a virtuous man."

"Would you like me to go?"

"No," he said, sliding his hand further up her thigh. "I like being corrupted by my wife."

She began loosening his tie. "This doesn't seem very comfortable," she commented, "if you want your spirits lifted."

"Or anything else," he murmured.

She swallowed a laugh. She finished with the tie and deftly opened the top button of his shirt. She felt deliciously wanton, sitting here seducing the big boss in his office.

She caught the muted glimmer of an antique silver chain. Her stomach made a sickening lurch. With trembling fingers she unbuttoned another button, another one, her breath lodged in her throat. Her hand stilled, her body froze. There it lay, nestled amid the soft whorls of dark chest hair.

The silver sailboat.

Amy felt reality shattering the protective bubble of her illusion, bringing to an end the enchanted fairy tale of the past few weeks.

She had known it could not last, had hoped and prayed it would. But the truth of her life with Michael could not be repressed forever. There would be reminders, hiding in corners, in all sort of hidden places. Like the old silver disc she was looking at now.

Grief, like jagged glass, cut through her. *No,* she thought, *please, no. Not this. Not now.* Tears, hot and painful, blurred her vision.

"Amy, what's wrong?" He caught her chin in his hand, made her face him. "You're crying," he said incredulously.

She shook her head, as if in denial, her throat clogged with emotion. She couldn't speak.

As if by instinct, he reached up to his chest, to where her hands had been a moment ago. He caught the disc in his palm. "Is it this? Should I not have worn it?"

"I'm sorry," she whispered. "I didn't expect to see it."

"I found it in a hidden pocket in my briefcase this morning. It had escaped my attention before. It's beautiful."

So it was. Beautiful and one of a kind, specially crafted by an artist on St. Barlow. A sailboat was engraved on the front of the disc. On the back was a date.

He let it slip out of his hand and it settled back against his chest. "I was going to ask you about it tonight."

"I gave it to you." *Don't ask me why,* she pleaded silently, fighting tears. Would the pain never end?

He wrapped his arms around her, holding her close. "I'm sorry," he said. "I didn't know, I didn't—"

She needed diversion, something innocent to say before he would ask the questions she didn't want to answer. Not now, not yet. "We did a lot of sailing on the island," she said tremulously. It was true enough. She tried to scramble off his knees, needing distance, wanting to get away, to hide in a dark corner and cry her heart out. His arms around her held her down.

"Don't go," he said quietly. "Talk to me, Amy."

She shook her head, face down. "I have to go home, please."

He drew her cheek against his. "Amy, don't keep things from me. Tell me, please."

"I can't. Please...please let me go."

She slid off his lap, searched nervously for her shoe that had fallen off her foot. She found it under the desk and slipped it on.

He'd come to his feet as well and caught hold of her hand. "Amy, you're upset. Please don't go. Tell me what's wrong."

"I'm just being over-emotional," she said thickly. "I'll be all right. Really."

He regarded her with concern. "I love you, Amy," he said softly.

New tears threatened. "I know." Blindly, she hurried out of the office.

Michael stared at the open file on the desk in front of him, thinking about Amy.

She was hiding something from him.

In the two days since she'd run out of his office crying, she'd tried to act as if nothing had happened. He'd given her every chance to reopen the subject of the sailboat, but she had clearly not wanted to discuss it.

At night, in bed, she clung to him, and he'd sensed a desperate, frenzied quality to her lovemaking—as if she were afraid of something.

She *was* afraid of something. He'd caught the fear in her face on several occasions in the last couple of days.

He took the silver disc out of his desk drawer and examined it again, as he had done several times now, willing himself to remember. Turning it over, he contemplated the date engraved on the back. It meant nothing to him—not his birthday, not their wedding date.

Elbows braced on the desk, he pressed his hands against his face and waited for an image, a thought, a whisper of something to enter his consciousness.

There was nothing.

He flung the wretched thing back in the drawer and slammed it closed. "Damn, damn," he muttered between clenched teeth.

He shoved his chair back and came to his feet and paced restlessly around the room, hands balled into fists. He wanted to feel like a normal human being again. He wanted his memory back. He wanted his life back.

His memory was there, somewhere in his brain, mysteriously locked away. Why couldn't he remember the significance of a sailboat? Why didn't Amy want to tell him?

He stared at the phone on his desk, hesitated, then crossed the room and sat down again in his chair. He reached for the receiver, dialed, and waited.

"Russ? It's Michael." It felt odd to talk to this man who was supposed to be his best friend, but not to *feel* it. They'd spoken on several occasions, but the conversations had been awkward, characterized by a cheerfulness and camaraderie that seemed forced and unnatural.

"Michael! Good to hear from you. How are you?"

"Fine. Not much going on at the amnesia front, but it's not been long." He might as well get that news over with, since Russ would ask. "How is Melissa?"

"She's sick and tired of lying in bed all day. Getting restless, as you can imagine, but the doctors say everything is looking good and the baby is growing. So, how's Amy?"

"She's...fine." Michael rubbed his chin, hesitating. "There's something I wanted to ask you," he began. "Do you remember an antique silver disc on a chain I used to have? It has a sailboat engraved on it."

"Sure do. Amy had it made by an artist on St. Barlow a few years ago. Nice piece."

"There's a date on the back." Michael read it to Russ. "Any idea what that means?"

"Nope, no idea. Why don't you ask Amy?"

Michael struggled briefly with the temptation to tell Russ the truth, that Amy didn't want to talk about it, was hiding something from him.

"I'll do that," he said casually.

But he knew he wouldn't.

Amy shivered as she closed the sliding doors that led from the living room onto the wooden deck. It had suddenly turned stormy and dark, and a cold, damp wind swept through the open windows, tugging at curtains and papers lying on the table.

She didn't feel well, hadn't felt well for a couple of days. It wasn't physical, at least not the cause. She didn't know how long she could go on feeling

the heaviness in her chest, this awful sense of fore-
boding.

I'm here to help Michael, she told herself. *I made
a commitment and I've got to see it through.*

A sunny morning had turned into a threatening,
gloomy afternoon. She glanced up at the sky,
bruised with dark clouds the color of lead and pew-
ter, and felt a sense of doom. She shivered again.

In the bedroom she pulled on a sweatshirt.
Huddled on the sofa, she tried fruitlessly to read a
book and get her mind off her problems, but the
story failed to keep her attention. Impatiently she
came to her feet. It was too soon to start dinner
preparations, so she might as well empty the last two
boxes of books. Some of the other ones they'd done
together one evening. In spite of her cheerless mood,
she felt a smile creep around her mouth. They'd
found some interesting material to read to each
other.

She slid open the cartons with a sharp knife from
the kitchen and began to arrange the books on the
shelves. She recognized some of Michael's business
texts, some fun fiction she remembered reading herself, and a variety of travel guides.

And then she found herself looking at a book she
had refused to read, had thrown into a corner, crying
with rage. A book a well-meaning friend had sent
her.

Lightning slashed the sky, briefly lit up the room
in glaring unforgiving light.

Sitting on the floor, her body frozen, Amy stared
at the title on the cover.

GRIEVING, it said in large letters. *When You Lose
a Child*, in smaller letters underneath.

CHAPTER SEVEN

NOTHING in the world would ever soothe her pain and some fool had sent her a book, a *book*! She'd been livid, had hurled the offensive thing into a corner, too angry to even open it. What was she going to learn from a *book*! How could mere words on paper ever help? The anguish was so deep, nothing would ever touch it.

Amy sat on her knees on the rug, the book in her hand, and the feelings washed over her again, in all their raw, devastating power. The rain poured from the heavens, darkening the world outside, inside.

She'd been less than four months old, a cuddly, happy, healthy baby, a child they had treasured, watched bloom with awe and joy. The delighted gurgles, the sweet smiles, the tiny hands, gripping fingers, ears, hair.

"She's a miracle," Michael had said once, watching her with love and wonder. "I never knew, I never knew..."

Then the unimaginable had happened.

There had been no warning, no reason.

She'd simply died in her sleep, never awakened in the morning. Medical science had a name for it, if not an explanation: SIDS, or Sudden Infant Death Syndrome.

Amy didn't know how long she sat there, unmoving, with the book in her lap, feeling the pain tearing at her again, feeling the tears running soundlessly down her face.

She found herself leafing through the book, noticing that a corner of a page had once been folded, noticing pencil marks. Someone had read it.

Michael.

She had accused him of not caring, of not grieving the way she was grieving for the loss of their child. He'd gone on living the way he always had—going to work in the morning, spending his day managing and organizing and meeting people and making decisions. Coming home in the evening, he'd eat dinner, read the paper, never mentioning the baby, as if the baby had never existed at all.

Yet he had read the book she had refused to read.

Her gaze lingered on the words and sentences in the semi-darkness, drawn by an invisible force. What had he found in these pages?

She reached over and turned on a lamp. Still sitting on the floor, her back against the sofa, unable to fight a painful curiosity, she began to read, her gaze sliding warily over the sentences, paragraphs and pages.

She read, forgetting time, forgetting where she was. In many of the pages she found herself, recognized her emotions and reactions in the stories of others, recognized Michael and the man he had become, secluding himself in his office, burying himself in work, hiding his grief where no one would see it. After all, he was a man, and a man was supposed to be strong.

And so Amy learned that generally men do not grieve the way women grieve, that often in time of crisis husbands and wives do not understand each other. Instead of drawing them together, grief tears them apart.

And as she kept reading, the realization came to her that the tragedy of their broken marriage should never have happened, could have been avoided.

If only, if only…

She noticed after a while that the rain had stopped, that outside the sun was shining on a dripping world glistening with water-diamonds.

She heard a car drive up, the slamming of a door, then the front doorbell. Oh, no, she didn't want to see anybody right now. She glanced out the window and knew by the mop of dark curly hair that it was Kristin. She liked Kristin, but this was not the time to do some more female bonding over a cup of coffee. She simply wasn't up to it. Still, she had no choice but to open the door.

"Hi!" Kristin stood in front of her in jeans and a damp T-shirt, smelling of sea and fish. She thrust a plastic bag at Amy. "Thought you might like some. We've got more than we know what to do with. They're cleaned and scaled."

The bag had fish in it.

Amy forced down the hysterical little laugh that rose in her throat. "Oh, thank you," she managed to say, the habit of good manners coming to her rescue. "Come on in."

"No, no, I've got to run. Besides, I've got the kids and my parents in the car." She frowned, studying Amy's face. "Are you all right?"

"I'm fine," she lied, knowing it was obvious she wasn't.

Kristin hesitated, still assessing her. Someone

honked the car horn. "These kids! You try to teach them manners..." She grimaced in mock despair. "I've got to run and get myself sanitized for the party tonight." She backed away from the door. "You're coming, aren't you?"

Tonight. Amy struggled to clear her mind. The party. Of course. She hadn't given it a thought all day.

She nodded. "Yes, yes, we'll be there. I'll see you then, and thank you so much for these."

"Oh, you're welcome." Kristin rushed back to the car.

Amy emptied the bag in the kitchen sink. Two salmon. Their lifeless eyes stared up at her. What to do?

She couldn't think. Couldn't deal with fish and parties. All she could think of was Michael and how she had misunderstood him, how she had misjudged him and how, in the end, she had hated him.

She stood there staring at the dead fish in the sink with the tears pouring down her cheeks.

"I was beginning to despair," the man said to Michael, "that I would ever meet this mystery wife of yours." Darin Kramer was a handsome man in his forties with a greasy smile that made Amy recoil instantly. Apparently he was a local businessman who'd met with Michael before his accident.

"It is a pleasure to meet you, Amy," the man said, curiosity undisguised in his expression.

She shook his hand and smiled politely, suppressing the urge to rush off and wash her hands.

"You were a well-kept secret," he commented.

"Imagine that," Michael said dryly. "I forgot I

had a wife." He draped his arm around her in a possessive gesture. "It's a good thing she didn't forget about me."

His ability to joke about his affliction never ceased to amaze her. Her heart swelled with love. He was a strong man, and even this distressing situation was not going to get him down, she knew. He was hoping and coping and not giving in to despair—certainly he would not allow anyone to see his distress and frustration.

As no one had seen outward signs of his grief after the baby had died. Even she had never seen Michael cry, not once. "Men do not cry in public," the book had said. "They do not want to appear weak in front of others." Men cried alone, in the garage, in the car, in places where no one would see them.

Michael's arm tightened around her and she caught the warmth in his eyes as he glanced down into her face.

"Shall we get something to eat?" he asked, gesturing at the buffet table.

She nodded and he took her hand and led her across the room.

Had Michael ever cried alone? she wondered. Her heart ached at the thought. She had cried alone, and in public, and in front of her friends and Michael. She hadn't cared what anyone thought; she'd lost her baby. What else could possibly matter? She needed comfort and a listening ear.

Michael had tried, but she knew he did not like coming home to find her weeping. He did not like to talk about the baby. When she had needed him most, he had not been there for her.

Not because he had not cared. Not because he did not love her.

Because he had not known how to nurture her when he was devastated by his own grief. Michael, who could do anything, Michael, who found solutions for every problem that came his way, was hurting to the limits of his capacity and had been unable to comfort her.

"Amy! Michael!" Kristin, balancing an overflowing plate of food, stood in front of them, grinning. She had undergone a stunning metamorphosis and was now draped in a slinky white dress that made her look elegant and sophisticated. It was difficult to imagine she was the same person who, wet and smelling of fish, had stood at the door only hours earlier.

"The food is fabulous," Kristin said. "We'll be out on the terrace. Why don't you come and join us?" Hips swinging, she weaved herself deftly toward the open doors.

Amy scanned the table with the artistically displayed food. Delicious, all of it, she was sure, but she had little appetite. She felt strange, disconnected, as if part of her wasn't present—if she were in a sort of trance going through the motions.

"Is that all you want?" Michael asked, surveying the modest selection of food on her plate.

"I'll go back for more if I want it," she said evasively.

Outside, on the terrace, they joined Kristin and her husband at a table. Amy stared at her plate and forked up a marinated mushroom. The conversation drifted around her, her mind far away.

Later she felt Kristin's hand on her arm. "Are you

finished?'' she whispered. ''I want to talk to you.''
Amy came to her feet and followed her to a quiet
corner.

''I'm sorry I had to run this afternoon,'' Kristin
said, looking uneasy. ''I know you were...upset, and
I know it's none of my business and I'm really not
trying to pry, except—'' She drew in a noisy breath,
frowned, obviously searching for the right words.
''Except that I keep thinking that you're new in
town and with all that's going on with Michael
you're under a lot of stress and...'' She shrugged.
''Oh, shoot, what I'm trying to say, Amy, is that if
you need someone to talk to, I'm here.''

Amy felt a sudden lump in her throat. ''Thank
you,'' she said. ''I appreciate that.''

Kristin looked right at her. ''I mean it, really. You
know how it is with women—we need to talk and
cry and spill our emotions and we need someone to
listen and sympathize. Just give me a call, anytime,
okay?''

''Thank you. You're...very nice.''

Kristin's face broke into a grin. ''Tell my kids
that. They think I'm the Wicked Witch from the
West because I won't feed them pizza for dinner
three nights in a row.''

Amy managed a smile. ''That's pretty mean all
right. Their psyches will be damaged for the rest of
their lives.''

''And when they grow up they'll sue me, I know.
I'm lying awake nights.'' Kristin grabbed her hand.
''Come on, let's have some of that sinful chocolate
mousse.''

An hour later Amy had had enough of the festiv-
ities. She was not in the mood for laughter and fri-

volity and she wanted to go home. Watching Michael across the room, she felt her love for him like an ache in her chest, and out of nowhere an image flashed through her mind. Michael, bare-chested, holding a freshly bathed, naked Lizzie in his strong arms. How tiny she had looked cradled against that brown, muscled chest. And in her mind Amy saw again Michael's face as he'd gazed down at his baby daughter—an expression of indescrib-able wonder. "I never knew," he'd said softly, "that I could love something this little this much."

It had been a moment of such perfection that Amy knew she would never forget it. Yet she had not thought of this, or consciously remembered it for a very long time. Amy thought now of all the things she had read in the book, all the things that suddenly made such sense to her now. How could she have had so little understanding of the man she loved?

She stared blindly at a wildly colored painting on the wall, felt an arm come around her.

"I was looking for you," Michael said, drawing her close against his side. "What are you doing here all by yourself?"

"Just looking at the painting." She leaned her head against his shoulder.

"You've been rather quiet this evening," he said, "and you hardly had anything to eat. Are you feel-ing all right?"

She was touched by the concern in his voice. "I'm fine," she said, her voice catching. "Just not very hungry. What do you think of this painting?"

"Mmm. It's rather ferocious. I wouldn't hang it in the bedroom."

"No." She faked a little shiver. "It might cause

nightmares.'' It felt good standing here with him, her head against his shoulder, like it belonged there. How was it possible she had ever thought she no longer loved him?

"Let's go home," she said.

He smiled at her. "Best offer I've had all night."

In bed she curled up against him. "Just hold me," she whispered.

Amy took the package wrapped in white out of the drawer and put it on the bed. The white plastic bag had been sealed shut with several lengths of wide tape.

Sitting on her knees in front of the bed, she lifted a piece of tape at the corner and slowly ripped it off the plastic bag. Then another one and another one.

The room was quiet, the open window letting in the scent of pines and the chirping of birds. Such peacefulness surrounding her, such turmoil in her heart.

She crumpled the tape into small balls. The bag was open now. She slipped her hand inside and drew out the white album. She tossed the bag on the floor and made herself look at the book on the bed in front of her.

The cover had a design of flowers and butterflies in soft baby colors. She gently laid her hand on the cover and stroked it. Her heart raced.

Open it, she admonished herself. *Open it. Look at the pictures.* She closed her eyes. Her greatest joy and greatest sorrow lay caught on paper in the images between the covers of the album. All she had to do was look.

She couldn't do it.

She wasn't ready.

She couldn't bear to see the photos. Not now, not today.

She dreamed of the baby that night, a nightmare full of black terror and she woke up screaming.

She was sitting upright in bed, heart pounding, and felt Michael's arms come around her. "It's all right," he said soothingly. "It's all right. I'm here."

She gulped in air, wiped at her face, wet with tears. *Oh, God,* she thought, *not again.*

She'd had the nightmare many times before, but not in the last year. A tremor went all through her and she pressed her face against the warmth and comfort if his neck. "I'm sorry," she whispered.

"You were screaming. Did you have a nightmare?"

She took in another deep breath, trying to calm herself. "Yes, but I'm awake now. I'll be all right." It would help to get up, to have something to drink, watch something innocuous on television—anything that might chase away the terrible images in her mind.

"Do you want to talk about it?" he asked softly.

She shook her head. "I just want it to go away." She moved out of his embrace and sat up in bed. "I'll go get a drink of water."

"I'll get it for you." He threw back the covers and she put a hand on his arm to hold him back.

"No, no, I need to move around a bit, be up for a while." She slid out of bed and went into the kitchen and made a cup of tea. She curled up on the sofa and turned on the TV.

"You have such beautiful eyes," the young man

said to the skinny girl on the screen. "I sense a great sadness. What tortures your soul?"

"You," said the girl, and sauntered away, snapping her gum.

Amy clicked the remote control, channel surfing, hoping to find something to engage her mind on some minimal level.

A dog food commercial. A doomsday discussion about water pollution. She clicked the remote control. A car chase, sirens screaming. It was hopeless. She turned off the TV and sipped her tea.

Michael came into the room. He sat down next to her and stroked her cheek. "Drink up and come back to bed," he said. "I'm lonely."

"Okay," she said obediently.

In bed he wrapped himself around her and she fell asleep almost instantly.

Later, something stirred her to semi-consciousness. She sighed and turned around. Michael was not in bed. Music, somewhere. She drifted off for a moment, stirring again uneasily. Such sad music. She opened her eyes. The room was in darkness, and the air seemed to tremble with a strange energy.

She listened to the music, feeling fear creeping through her.

Michael was playing the piano, and the notes exuded a dark despair that reached straight into her soul. She had never heard him play like this, play with such anguish and sorrow.

She slipped out of bed, pulled on a robe and went into the living room. He was sitting in the dark, playing without music, without light, playing as if he had lost his soul.

Maybe he had.

She stood beside him, saw the tormented lines of his back and shoulders. His eyes were closed and the music poured out of his fingers, his body—a torrent of loss and pain.

Then suddenly he stopped, sitting rigid and still, head bent, his eyes still closed.

Amy could feel the tension in the room, the music still vibrating in the air, still tingling along her nerves. Moving behind him, she gently laid her hands on his shoulders, needing to touch him, to feel him, to somehow comfort him.

He swiveled around on the stool, wrapped his arms around her waist and pressed his face against her breasts. He was trembling against her.

"Michael, what's wrong?" she whispered.

"I don't know," he said tonelessly. "I don't know what came over me. Where all this came from."

For a few minutes they held each other in silence. Then he straightened, sliding his hands from her back to the sides of her breasts. She felt the heat of him against her, flowing out of his hands, his body.

"Let's go back to bed," he said thickly.

He made love to her with a desperate passion that almost frightened her. His intensity was overpowering, his mouth and hands hungry, greedy. His fierceness stunned her into helplessness, but not for long. The flames of an answering craving sprang up inside her, consumed her like a fever. Her body tangled with his, her mind intoxicated by thrilling sensations of blind, naked hungering, wanting more, more...

He lifted his face, his body trembling. "Amy..."

It was a plea. His eyes were a tarnished gold and she recognized in them the nameless anguish taunting him from the depths of forgetting. Breathless, frenzied, the tension almost unbearable inside her, she reached up to cradle his face in her hands.

"I love you," she whispered, and she heard his muffled groan of release and felt herself slipping, falling over the edge into oblivion.

They didn't speak for a long time.

"Promise me something," he said finally, still holding her close against him. "Promise me you won't leave me."

"Michael...I love you."

"Please," he said huskily, "even if I never get my memory back, don't leave me. Promise me."

She closed her eyes. "I'll never leave you," she whispered.

CHAPTER EIGHT

MICHAEL fell asleep almost instantly and Amy listened to his breathing. She remembered the day she had decided to leave him, the day she had simply packed two suitcases, taken a cab to the airstrip and boarded the puddle jumper that had flown her off the island.

The night before she and Michael had attended a business cocktail party. She'd moved around like a sleep walker, not having the mental strength to be polite and smile and make friendly conversation. Nothing much mattered anymore, nothing but the pain of losing her baby.

And then she'd caught sight of Michael standing in a corner with her friend Sasha and a couple of other people she didn't know.

Michael was laughing. Laughing out loud, head thrown back.

It was such a shocking, unfamiliar sight that for a moment she forgot to breathe. His distant, unemotional expression had vanished miraculously, and he seemed carefree and happy. She could not help staring, seeing and hearing nothing around her but Michael and the few people with him.

The laughter went on. Something was apparently hugely funny—probably one of Sasha's stupid goat stories—and it was feeding on itself because there seemed no end to the laughter. It filled her head like the roaring of the sea.

Feet rooted to the floor, Amy stared at Michael's happy face, felt herself fill up with a burning rage. How dare he? How dare he laugh? How dare he have fun while their lives lay shattered to pieces!

He doesn't care! she thought wildly. *He's a monster!*

She ran. Away from Michael and the laughter, away from the noise and the people as if pursued by an invisible evil. She stormed out into the dark night, only semi-conscious of moving, fueled by anger and anguish.

Running, running.

She became aware suddenly that she had left the hotel grounds and was hiking down the road, walking in her bare feet. She didn't know where she was going. She was just moving, putting one foot in front of the other while tears streamed down her face.

She lost all sense of time and direction. Finally, out of breath, she collapsed on a wooden bench by a deserted food stall. It was a dark night with only a sliver of a moon peeking through the palm fronds above her head. She didn't know where she was and she didn't care. She noticed in an absent sort of way that her feet were bleeding, and she didn't care about that either. All she saw in her mind was the image of Michael laughing, laughing.

How long since they'd last laughed? How long since she'd felt happy? Would she ever feel happy again?

Then there were bright lights. A car stopped and Michael was coming toward her and she heard herself screaming at him. She hated him and never wanted to see him again. He didn't care that the baby had died. He didn't care about her and her feelings and she wanted him to leave her alone.

He did not leave her alone. Somehow he managed to maneuver her into the car and drive her home and all during the ride she cried hysterically and accused him of all manner of horrible things. He said nothing, not a single word, and by the time they arrived at the house she was finished raging and felt as limp as a dirty dishrag.

The house was empty and quiet; the housekeeper had left hours earlier.

"Sit," he ordered when they entered the living room.

She sat. She had no energy left to do anything else. Nothing in his face now gave away that he'd been laughing and enjoying himself earlier that evening. He seemed as alien and distant as a stranger from another continent.

"Where are your shoes?" he asked.

"I don't know." She must have taken them off and left them by the road somewhere. Expensive, high-heeled Italian shoes and she didn't care if she ever saw them again.

He brought a plastic pan of warm water, towels, a first-aid kit. "Soak your feet in the water," he said, and she did so obediently.

She felt numb, her mind occupied now with noticing irrelevant details such as the color of the plastic pan—blue—and the tiny red light on the CD player, and the high-pitched sound of the tree frogs outside.

She watched without feeling anything as Michael washed her feet, applied ointment and bandaged them. She observed his hands—strong, capable hands that could fix anything, hands that had once saved a small boy from drowning. She saw his hands like she saw any casual object in her surroundings— a lamp, a candlestick. She watched as he cleared everything away. He was a handsome man, even now with his expression so remote and stern. She felt no connection, no love, nothing.

Finished with his ministrations, he lowered his tall frame in a chair across from her. Leaning forward, he rested his elbows on his thighs and clasped his hands between his knees. "So," he said slowly, "you took off because you were upset because I was laughing."

"Yes." She stared at the little red light on the CD player. "I suppose Sasha was telling one of her stupid goat stories," she said bitterly.

"As a matter of fact, yes. You are quite a fan of those stories yourself."

"Well, not anymore," she snapped, still avoiding his gaze.

"You haven't laughed for a very long time," he said softly.

She gave him a hateful look. "I don't *feel* like laughing. You may not understand that, but that's just how it is."

He was silent for a while.

"Amy," he said finally, his voice low, "it felt *good* to laugh again. Should I feel guilty?"

"Do you?" She looked right into his eyes. She saw a flicker of pain, or was she imagining it?

"I did, yes. But it isn't rational, Amy—"

"Rational?" she asked with cold mockery. "Is that what you're concerned with? *Rational?* Tell me what's rational about what happened! Tell me in what way it made any sense at all! *Then* I'll worry about being rational!''

He rubbed his face and sighed. "Amy, we can't keep asking ourselves why. There is no answer. There never will be an answer. But we can't hang onto the past and let it consume us; we've got to go on, Amy. We've got to move on with our lives!''

The sudden vehemence in his voice shook her and anger rushed to the surface again.

"Well, you're doing a fine job of it, by the looks of it,'' she said scathingly. "I don't imagine you ever even think about her anymore.'' She lurched to her feet, wincing at the pain in her feet, suddenly sharp and stinging. "Go ahead, party, have fun. By all means, don't let the past consume you.''

She stumbled to her room, the room they no longer shared, threw herself on the bed and lay there, dry-eyed until she fell into an exhausted sleep.

The next day she packed her bags, wrote Michael a note, and flew back to Philadelphia.

Now, two years later, in the dawn-colored room on the Oregon coast, Amy watched Michael sleeping next to her in the bed and knew with searing regret that leaving him had been the worst decision of her life.

The next morning, Amy once again took the baby album out of the drawer and looked at the cover. Again her hand began to tremble, her heart began to pump in distress.

Again she hid the album in the drawer, unopened.

I need time, she thought. *I just need some more time.*

But time she did not have.

Glancing at the calendar later that morning, she realized to her horror that school would start in three days.

Amy sank down on a kitchen chair and covered her face with her hands. "Oh, no," she muttered to herself. "Three days!"

How could she have let it go so far without even thinking about it? Thousands of miles away, she had a life in Philadelphia. A life that somehow had faded into the background of her consciousness, but it was real, very real.

She was a teacher. She had a small, but nice, apartment; had friends with whom she did the usual things—shopping, going to the movies, eating out.

On the surface it was not a bad life, but behind this pleasant façade her existence was cold and empty. Her friends did not know she was divorced, did not know that, for a brief time, she had been a mother.

In the last couple of years she'd tried hard not to think about her life—she'd more or less just lived it from day to day, going to work, filling her free time with busyness.

Amy rubbed her face and gave a low moan. It was time now to do some thinking about that life, to remember she had obligations, an apartment with rent due, a friend who watered her plants and had no idea where she was and might be worried.

She was living here as Michael's wife, pretending she had no other life, but this could not go on. Something had to happen. Something had to be decided.

Three days.

The school doors would open, the kids would

pour in. She was supposed to be there to teach. That was expected of her; that was her life.

She sucked in a deep breath. She had to decide what she wanted.

She already knew what she wanted.

She wanted her husband back.

She got up and paced restlessly through the kitchen while wisps of misty thought struggled for consciousness.

Carefully, slowly, she allowed herself to form the thoughts fully in her mind, to shape them into words.

I can quit my job and break the lease on my apartment.

Her heart began to hammer wildly.

It was pure madness to think this way, to give up everything—work, money, friends, security, independence.

She stared out over the ocean, hearing Michael's voice floating into her mind. *Don't leave me. Promise me.*

She knew what she had to do.

Two hours later she had resigned from her job, canceled the lease on her apartment, made arrangements for her furniture and personal belongings to be put in storage, and was talking on the phone to a distressed and worried Mack, her friend and neighbor who'd taken in her mail and watered her plants.

"Amy! Where have you been! I was about to file a missing person's report! Where are you?"

She told him where she was. She told him what she had done that morning.

"Are you nuts? What are you *thinking*! Why

didn't you talk to me first! You could have sublet your place! And why resign from your job? Wouldn't they give you a leave of absence? Did you ask?"

"No," she said.

"Why not?"

"Because I don't belong in Philadelphia."

I belong here, she thought silently. *I belong with Michael.*

She felt a sudden light, floating sense of euphoria and everything felt beautifully, radiantly right.

She'd expected that, after the reality of what she had done had settled in, panic would strike. It did not.

She cooked a special dinner, bought flowers for the table, put on a flirty little dress.

"You look...ravishing," Michael said when he came home, smiling. "Are we going out?"

She shook her head, putting her arms around his neck. "No. I just felt like celebrating."

"Celebrating what?"

"Us." She touched her mouth to his. "You and me," she whispered against his lips.

Later that evening they sat on the sofa watching a movie on television, something rather light and fluffy that required little of their attention. They were focussing mostly on each other and the wonderful things their hands could do.

On the screen two small girls were jumping up and down on an old wooden bed, shrieking with laughter. The frame was making creaky noises of protest and the inevitable happened: the bed collapsed under their feet and the girls crumpled on top of each other, breathless with laughter.

"We crashed through a bed once," Amy said, feeling instant delight at the memory. "It was quite...exciting."

He cocked a suspicious brow. "And how did we do that? Jump up and down?"

"No." She pursed her lips teasingly, not elaborating.

"Are you going to tell me or do I have to drag it out of you?" he said. "Where was this? When did this happen?"

"All right, all right," she said, straightening her back and taking a dramatic breath in preparation for telling the story. "It was a year after we were married. We were in the States on vacation and we were going to visit friends in Louisiana and our rental car broke down right in front of this tatty little motel." She grinned. "So we decided to spend the night there and deal with the car the next day."

"And we crashed through the hotel bed?" Michael frowned, apparently trying to see if a spark of recognition dawned. "How did we do that?"

"We were sort of eh...wrestling."

He arched his brows. "Wrestling?"

"Well, you know, you were trying to seduce me, and...eh..."

"I was *trying* to seduce you? Was that a big struggle?" His tone was dry. So far he had not been presented with much struggle from her when he wanted to make love.

"I didn't want to." The incredulous expression on his face almost made her giggle. "And you sort of threw me on the bed and you fell on top of me and the whole thing just went down."

"You didn't *want* to?" he asked, as if the fact of

the crashing through the bed was not nearly as amazing as the fact that she had not wanted his amorous attentions.

She looked at him demurely. "Well, you know, I had a headache, and I was tired."

"And you probably just had your hair done, too," he added dryly.

She nodded. "Yes, that too." She sighed. "So I begged you not to."

"You *begged* me?"

"Yes. I said, 'Please, Michael, not tonight. Please, no, no. *Please*.'"

"Oh, I see. So I *wrestled* with you, trying to *force* myself on you?"

She bit her lip, but she knew she couldn't keep the laughter out of her eyes. "Well, a man has his needs."

He groaned and rolled his eyes. "Why are you making up this ridiculous story?"

"I'm not making it up. It happened." She laughed; she couldn't stop herself. "Except that it was all make-believe. I was only *pretending* I had a headache and was tired. It was just a game."

"That's a good thing, because I was beginning to get seriously concerned there for a minute."

Not for a very long minute, she was quite sure.

He was still observing her, his face brooding. "And why were you playing a game?"

"We had to do *something*. The place was a dump and there wasn't even a television. Anyway, I started it. I pretended to resist your...eh...amorous overtures."

"And why would you want to do that? So far I've

found that you're quite happy with my romantic advances.''

She chuckled. "You are so sure of yourself, aren't you? I did it because you always think you can just snap your fingers and I'm all yours and—''

"I do *not* snap my fingers, and I don't believe I ever did!''

"Figuratively speaking, of course," she said a touch haughtily. "Anyway, once in a while it won't hurt you to have to work for it a little, you know, just to keep you on your toes.''

Before he could respond to that, she managed to slip away from his arm and raced out the door. He went after her in a flash of a moment. She ran out into the garden, heading for the woods, but he caught up with her and captured her in his embrace before she made it out the gate.

"I'll teach you not to play games with me," he said darkly.

She struggled against him, almost breathless, laughing, until she gave it up and went limp in his arms. He began to kiss her, lowering her onto the grass—soft and cool against her bare arms and legs.

He lay on top of her, nuzzling her neck, driving her wild. "You're not going to escape me now," he whispered in her ear. "I'm going to ravish you right here and now.''

"If you want to be Neanderthalish about this, I guess I have no choice. I'll just suffer through it.''

"You'll enjoy every little minute of it," he said smugly, and proceeded to prove it.

There was no time for finesse, for long leisured loving. It was too late for that. Fire and wildness and passion consumed them, until the tension shattered and their bodies shuddered into stillness once more.

For a long time they lay in each other's arms, under the stars.

"I hope," he said softly, "that you didn't suffer too much."

She couldn't help but chuckle at his triumph. "You're so bad," she said.

He flashed her a cocky grin. "No, you've got it all wrong, sweetheart. I'm *good*."

She dropped her face onto his chest and groaned. "I give up."

"Good. Now let's go inside. It's getting cold."

They crawled under the covers of their big, comfortable bed. She lay cuddled up against him, feeling his hand stroking her hip. He was staring up at the ceiling.

"After we crashed through the bed," he said slowly, "after we'd stopped laughing, we dragged the mattress off the broken frame, put it on the floor and made love. The curtains were open. Flowered curtains, and there was a full moon, shining straight down at us."

Amy was hardly breathing. "Yes," she whispered.

He turned his face to hers, his eyes full of warmth and love. "I remember that night. I remember what I was thinking."

"What?"

"I remember thinking the corporation I worked for owned luxury hotels with luxury beds the whole world over, available to me at any time, and the only place I wanted to be at that moment was right there in that shabby little room on a mattress on the floor, with you in my arms. I remember I felt like the happiest man in the world.''

"I'm starving," said Amy, plonking herself down on a big rock.

It was Sunday and they'd hiked deep into the woods, far away from the sounds of people and cars and telephones. They'd found an idyllic spot by a stream babbling happily over rocks and boulders and Amy gazed longingly at the crystal-clear water sparkling in the sunlight.

Michael grinned at her as he swung the backpack to the ground. "Don't even think about it," he said, reading her thoughts.

She sighed. "I know, I know. It's barely above freezing."

Michael sat down next to her and they plundered the backpack which held a treasure of Italian sandwiches, peaches and toasted hazelnuts.

Her hunger stilled, Amy felt a sweet lethargy take over and she lay back, bundling her sweatshirt under her head. She closed her eyes, dozing. The sound of the water rushing along in the stream had a soporific effect and for a while she slept, until she felt Michael's hand taking hers. She peered at him through her lashes.

He was sitting up, gazing down at her. He'd taken off his T-shirt and she enjoyed looking at him—his broad chest, tanned and strong, his legs long and muscular—all sexy male against the backdrop of ancient forest. She glanced up at his face, seeing the thoughtful expression, feeling a twinge of apprehension. She recognized that look. While she'd been dozing he'd been struggling with thoughts and feelings.

"Did I wake you?" he asked.

"Not really. I was just sort of blissing out." She squeezed his hand. "What are you thinking?"

He hesitated for a moment, his gaze sliding away from her face. "I've been wondering why all this is happening to us," he said then, staring up into the leafy canopy. "I can't help but wonder. I should be dead, and I'm not. It's my memory that's dead."

Amy's heart lurched at his words and the last of her languor vanished. She sat up and put her hand on his leg. "But it's coming back, Michael, little by little. It's only been a few weeks."

"Yes, but sometimes I get this...notion, this feeling that there's a reason behind it...a purpose. Does that sound crazy?"

"No." Amy swallowed uneasily. "A friend of mine is fond of saying that everything that happens to you happens for a reason. That there's a lesson to be learned from it."

As she said the words, she realized suddenly how true it was, at least for her—how much she had learned about herself and about the man she loved since she'd come to Oregon.

"So what am I supposed to learn?" he asked, frowning. "If I don't know what it is, what difference does it make?"

"I don't know. I don't think anyone else can tell you. Maybe figuring it out takes time too."

"Maybe." He was watching her, shadows in his eyes. "I do get the feeling sometimes that there's something I don't remember because I'm not *supposed* to remember, at least not yet."

Her heart skipped a beat. She clasped her hands together in her lap. "What do you mean you're not *supposed* to?"

"I don't know—just some crazy notion. Or maybe I don't remember it because I don't *want* to remember it." He shrugged, silent for a moment. "I read about a kind of amnesia caused by emotional trauma, something so devastating and painful you can't deal with it and so you simply banish it from your memory."

Amy grew utterly still. "You had an accident, Michael. It was physical trauma." Her voice shook.

"I know." He studied her face. "But there's something you haven't told me, isn't that right, Amy?" His voice was low, and she knew it wasn't really a question. He knew.

Fear locked her throat. *Don't ask me, please don't ask me to tell you.*

He lifted her clenched hands from her lap and gently untangled her fingers. "Amy? What is so terrible that you can't tell me?"

She forced down the fear. She needed to be calm. "I want you to get your memory back, Michael, but..." She closed her eyes. *I don't want to lose you,* she finished silently.

"But what?" he urged gently.

"I'm scared," she whispered. *I'm scared you'll hate me.*

"Why? What frightens you about my getting my memory back?"

She drew in an unsteady breath. "Because...the things you'll remember aren't all going to be happy and funny."

His eyes did not leave her face. "And you've

been trying very hard to tell me only the uplifting things to make me feel good.''

She nodded wordlessly.

"I know you have, Amy, but you don't have to protect me. It wouldn't be realistic to assume that I had a perfect life, I know that. I know I must have my share of unhappy memories. I must have made mistakes, done things I regretted, made people angry.''

"So have I," she said, not looking at him. She picked up the half-empty can of cola and took a drink, hoping they'd get off the subject.

"So, why don't you tell me the sordid stuff? Let's get it over with?''

"The good stuff is much more fun," she said, her voice nervous. "Besides, I don't want you to know my dark side.''

"All your sides are sunny, sweet and sexy. I'm your husband; I know.''

"You're wrong." She began stuffing the remnants of lunch in the backpack, avoiding his eyes.

He took the backpack away from her and put his hand under her chin, lifting her face to his. "You told me your morals were sterling.''

"Maybe I lied.''

He chuckled. "I find the idea that you have a dark side rather…interesting. So what did you do? Rob a bank? Run guns to a banana republic?''

"No." *I was not a good wife. I broke the most important promise I ever made and left you*, she wanted to say, but the words wouldn't come.

He kissed her softly. "Maybe you're a witch putting spells on people. Maybe you've put a spell on me?''

Tears burned behind her eyes and she twisted her face away from his hand and lowered her gaze. "Please, Michael, don't." Reaching for the backpack again, she tossed in the last of their things.

There was a silence and she could feel his regard like a touch, searching for meaning in her face.

"Amy, I don't want you keeping things from me. I have the right to know."

"Yes, you do." She focussed on fastening the buckle. Her hands shook. "I'll tell you," she said, "when...when I... can...when the time is right. I promise." She abandoned the wayward buckle.

"Here, let me do it," he offered, taking the backpack from her.

As his hands easily closed the backpack, Michael watched Amy wander closer to the stream, kneel down and wash her hands. He had noticed the terror in her eyes, seen her shaking hands, and he felt the shadow of something terrible settling over him.

CHAPTER NINE

IN THE days that followed, Amy could not shake the awful sense of impending doom. She was having trouble sleeping. *I need to tell him,* she kept thinking. *I need to tell him.*

She wanted desperately to have somebody to talk to, but she couldn't imagine who. Her friends in Philadelphia didn't know the truth and weren't close enough; the ones on the island she had deserted without telling them even where she was going. She called her mother in Madrid, where it was evening and was told by the housekeeper her parents were out.

Kristin.

She didn't know Kristin that well, but she was a nice person and she had offered. Amy reached for the phone.

Half an hour later Kristin stood at the door wearing old sweatpants and a T-shirt, her thick curly hair pulled back into an untidy ponytail. "Hope this isn't a dressy affair," she said lightly.

"Just coffee," said Amy, as if a serious answer was expected. She felt strangely uneasy. She poured them each a cup of coffee, and they sat down at the kitchen table to drink it. Kristin reached out and touched Amy's hand. "Spill it, kid."

Amy dragged in a fortifying gulp of air. "Please don't tell anybody about this."

"Not a soul."

Amy bit her lip, closed her eyes, opened them again and looked at Kristin. "Michael and I aren't married; we're divorced," she blurted out.

Kristin's expression did not change. "And Michael does not know this," she said evenly, apparently not at all surprised.

Amy stared at her. "You knew?"

Kristin spooned sugar into her coffee. "Not exactly. I knew there was something not quite…as it seemed. Everybody at the Aurora has been talking about it, Amy."

Amy felt her heart sink. "Everybody? What…what are they saying?"

"That something isn't kosher. Michael was here alone for a week or so before the accident. Everyone who met him then was under the impression he was single. There was no mention of a wife on his cv, and he actually told some people he wasn't married."

"Oh, no," Amy moaned, and buried her face in her hands. She thought of Julia, and Darin Kramer. What had made her think she could keep the truth a secret? She lifted her face. "Has anybody said anything to Michael?"

Kristin stirred her coffee slowly. "I doubt it. It's rather a delicate subject and nobody knows him well enough, besides, he has your wedding photo in his office now. And he's obviously totally gaga over you, so what is anybody going to say?"

Amy gave a nervous little laugh. "Gaga?"

Kristin grinned. "Okay, besotted, smitten, in love. He's nuts about you. Don't tell me you haven't noticed," she added wryly.

"This is all such a mess."

"Because he loves you?"

"No, yes. And...because I love him."

Kristin's mouth twitched. "He loves you, you love him. I can see you have a big problem here."

"The problem is that he doesn't remember the truth about our relationship."

Kristin looked penitent. "Sorry, I didn't mean to be flippant. It must be a terrible feeling not to know your own past."

"That's why he fell in love with me again, because he doesn't know, and..." Her voice faded out.

"Amy?" Kristin's voice was soft. "Just tell me, just let it out. I might not be able to help, or even to understand, but I can listen."

So Amy told Kristin the story, but not the whole story. She began saying that a few years ago their marriage had fallen apart and that she'd left Michael and divorced him. Kristin listened without interrupting as Amy told her about the phone call from Melissa, about getting on a plane to help Michael, about giving up her job and apartment in Philadelphia to stay with him.

"And Michael doesn't know any of this?" Kristin asked when Amy stopped talking.

Amy shook her head. "He thinks we're happily married."

"By all appearances, you are."

"Because he doesn't remember how bad it was."

Kristin searched her face. "And you're worried about him remembering again and that he'll stop loving you," Kristin said quietly

"Yes." Her throat ached and she swallowed. "And he senses something isn't right; he told me he knows I haven't told him everything."

"So what do you think you should do?"

"I don't know...I can't stand myself half the time."

"What do you mean?"

"I'm not honest with him and I hate all the deception. I can't go on living a lie." She blew out a strangled breath. "I know I have to tell him, but...I'm terrified."

Kristin looked thoughtfully into her coffee cup, as if answers were to be found on the bottom. "He loves you now, Amy," she said, looking up. "That might well make a difference."

It was a nice thought, but Amy was too afraid to hope, too afraid because she knew how it had once been.

"Hey," said Kristin softly. "I don't know what happened between you two, and you don't need to tell me, just ask yourself if it was truly unsolvable or unforgivable."

Amy shook her head. "Not anymore. Not for me."

"Then there's hope." Kristin leaned back in her chair. "Let's see, now. You know you love him. You know you can't keep living a lie. You know you have to level with him. So, what do you need me for?"

Amy gave her a wan smile. "As you said, I needed you to listen, for moral support." She made a face. "And if he doesn't want me anymore and I have to get out of here, I'll need a place to stay."

"One piece of advice," Kristin said. "If you love him, don't leave, no matter what."

*   *   *

"Your mail, sir," Mrs. Applegate said as she placed a bundle of sorted paperwork on Michael's desk. On top lay a blue envelope, intact, the address handwritten. "This one appears personal," she added, tapping it with a pink-polished nail, "so I didn't open it."

"Thank you."

The letter came from St. Barlow. He slit the envelope open and out slipped a note and several photos. The note was from Sasha.

> Sorry it took so long to get these to you. These were taken at your goodbye party and I marked everybody's name on the back, so you'll know.

He studied the first of the pictures. He recognized himself, sitting amid a group of people around a restaurant table, eating and laughing. Another snapshot showed everybody dancing, a steel band in the background. There were three more photos and they all had one thing in common. Amy wasn't in any of them. Jennifer Casey was in all of them.

He felt icy cold.

He pushed the pictures back in the envelope. He glanced at his watch and reached for the phone and dialed Russ's number.

"I need a straight answer," he said without preamble as soon as Russ came on the line.

"I'll give it my best. Shoot."

"Who is Jennifer Casey?"

"No idea. Never heard of her."

Michael closed his eyes and rubbed his neck. "Well, I guess that's as straight as it comes."

"Why do you want to know?"

Michael hesitated for a moment, then opted for straightforward as well. "I don't have any memory of this but it seems that I was having an affair with her before I came to Oregon."

There was a pregnant silence. "I think," Russ said carefully, "that you should have a talk with Amy. Tell her what you think."

Michael grimaced. It sounded like a terrible idea to him.

All day the photos haunted him.

Coming home, he found Amy in the kitchen tearing lettuce into a wooden salad bowl.

"How was your day?" she asked, smiling at him.

"Busy," he said, which was part of the truth. He loosened his tie, looking at her face. "Amy, have you ever heard of a Jennifer Casey?" He had not known he was going to ask the question, and for a moment he was terrified to hear his own words.

Amy's expression registered no recognition. She shook her head. "No. Who is she?"

"She did some work for the hospital on the island—computer network integration, or something like that."

Amy went back to tearing lettuce. "I never met her," she said.

"I'll go change my clothes." He walked out of the kitchen, not sure if he was relieved. If Jennifer had come to the island several times over a period of months to work at the hospital, had stayed at the hotel, how was it possible for Amy not to know who she was? By all accounts the island was tiny and visitors would no doubt be welcomed and entertained by the small expatriate community.

In the bedroom he tossed his tie on a chair,

shrugged out of his jacket and began unbuttoning his shirt, catching his reflection in the mirror. He stared at his greying hair, the serious set of his mouth, the strange shadows in his eyes, as he had done many times before. There was something not right, something that didn't *feel* right. He'd sensed it all along and it hadn't gone away as time went by. Instead, it was getting worse.

"Michael?" Amy entered the bedroom. "Are you all right?"

He shrugged impatiently. "I'm sick and tired of not remembering, of not knowing anything." He yanked off his shirt and threw it into the clothes hamper, using more force than was necessary, feeling the need to throw something, break something, to relieve his frustration. "I'm tired of waiting, of feeling so damned helpless! I detest being so consumed with myself, my life, my past sins. There are other things in this world I'd rather spend my energy on." He stalked into the bathroom, closing the door behind him, but not before he'd seen the fear in her eyes. He'd had enough of seeing that too, and knowing she wasn't telling him everything. He was tired of feeling guilty for transgressions he didn't even remember committing.

He splashed water on his face and tried to calm himself. Coming back into the bedroom, he found Amy gone. He changed into a pair of jeans and a T-shirt. She was in the kitchen fixing dinner and he paused in the door.

"I'm sorry I lost my cool," he said.

She didn't look at him, her eyes intent on the onion she was cutting. "It's all right, Michael. It's perfectly normal to get frustrated." Then she glanced up at him and smiled. "Don't worry about it. Have a drink and relax; dinner will be ready in twenty minutes."

He went to the living room and on impulse sorted through the various photo albums, finding the ones with what seemed to be the latest pictures taken. He examined the images carefully. Amy had long hair on all of them.

He studied himself. The man on the photos had laughing eyes, looked happy and carefree, and years younger than the man gazing back at him in the mirror. The present face was leaner, the features sharper, honed by some forgotten force.

Still, he'd noticed that it was better than it had been. He'd gained a few pounds and he looked less gaunt than even a couple of weeks ago.

He lifted out one of the snapshots and turned it over. A date was printed on the back, clearly readable. The print was four years old.

He took out several more, but all of them were from the same period.

He checked the other albums, but all the photos dated from even earlier times. He sat very still, trying to make sense of this information.

Four years and no photos? Not a single one?

"Dinner's ready," Amy announced, standing in the door to the living room. "Are you hungry?"

Her voice almost startled him, his mind far from thoughts of food. "Yes, yes," he said absently. He closed the photo album and pushed himself to his feet. He was aware suddenly of the tantalizing aromas wafting in from the dining room.

"It smells wonderful," he said, trying for normalcy.

They didn't speak much during dinner, although he said all the appropriate things about the food, which was delicious. Fresh salmon fillets poached in wine and herbs, a crisp salad and crusty country bread. She was a woman of many talents, this wife of his.

He watched her as she ate, observing her small hands, the curve of her chin, her slender neck, beautifully exposed below the gleaming cap of short hair. He watched her with a curious sense of detachment, afraid to feel, afraid to know.

Know what?

His chest felt tight. He swallowed another bite of food. A year from now, he thought, projecting into the future, what will our life be like?

Amy glanced up from her plate and smiled at him. Green eyes, clear, crystalline, yet so much lay concealed in their depths. So much those eyes had witnessed of which he remembered nothing—things she kept hidden from him. Her eyes were like the sea with all its secret, unseen life below the visible surface.

He should ask her about the photos, clear the air, but nameless fear kept him from broaching the subject. Perhaps he was better off not knowing.

"I have to check on something at the office," he told her later, after they'd had their coffee. "I won't be long." He felt relief as he left the house and took a deep breath of the pine-scented air. He headed quickly down the wooded path, entered his quiet office, and booted up his computer.

He didn't know what made him want to read

through his old e-mail messages again, the ones
from people on the island—a sudden irrepressible
impulse. Something had struck him as odd before,
but now, reading them again, he knew what it was.

There were no references to Amy. No one asked
how she was, no one told him to give her their love
or greetings.

The people on the island who had written him,
friends by all appearances, had not expected her to
be in Oregon with him. Not even after the accident.

He stared blindly at the screen. What had that
unsavory character Darin Kramer said not long ago?
Something about a mystery wife. And Julia
Morrison... He closed his eyes. *"You didn't tell me
you were married,"* she'd said, and he heard the
words clearly in his mind.

He grew very still, could hear the pounding of his
own heart.

He thought of that night when he'd held a screaming Amy in his arms, the night he couldn't go back
to sleep and found himself sitting at the piano, feeling an unknown anguish consuming him. Where had
all that misery come from? What had caused that
darkness in his soul? Why did he have the face of
a man who had no dreams left to dream?

Don't leave me, he had begged her.

He thought of the photo albums that contained no
pictures taken in the last four years.

Fear clutched at his heart, stealing his breath.

Amy prowled nervously through the house, waiting
for Michael to come back. She had not asked him
what he had to check at the office, but his mood had
been strange. The knot in her stomach seemed to get

tighter every day, taking up root like a parasite trying to strangle the life out of her.

The house was so quiet. It seemed a long time before she heard Michael's key in the lock.

He looked tired. His hair, windblown, fell over his forehead. She loved the lean, sporty look of him in his old faded jeans and the T-shirt hugging his broad shoulders. Loved it more when there was laughter in his eyes. There was none now.

"We need to talk," he said, raking a hand through his hair, pushing it back from his face.

Her stomach churned. "Is something wrong?" she asked. *Of course something is wrong,* she answered herself. *Everything is wrong.*

He lowered himself next to her on the sofa. "Sasha sent me a note with some photos of the goodbye party they put on for me," he said evenly. He fished them out of his pocket and handed them to her.

Amy stared at the happy images. Nothing special about them, just ordinary snapshots of people having fun. She knew many of them, had called them her friends.

"Why are you not in any of these pictures, Amy?" he asked.

Her heart racing, she scrambled for an answer. "I wasn't there. I'd already left," she said.

"Because of the hiking trip?"

She nodded. It was a blatant lie and she cringed, hating herself.

Leaning forward, he rested his arms on his thighs. "I was looking through the photo albums before dinner," he began. "The last pictures were taken four years ago.'' He paused, searching her face. ''Amy, where were you in the last four years?''

''The last four years?'' Her voice shook. ''I was on the island, with you.'' It was partially true; she'd left only two years ago.

''Why don't we have photos of you with your hair short? Or of me with my hair getting gray?''

She could feel the blood drain from her face and her mind scrambled for something, any kind of reasonable explanation.

The camera broke and I just never got around to buying a new one.

The albums got lost in a suitcase when we flew to Madrid to see my parents.

The albums were burned in a fire.

Deceit building on deceit. He'd see right through her. She didn't have it in her to try out these ridiculous, transparent lies.

''Amy?'' he urged.

She saw a terrible anguish in his eyes and her throat locked. Had he remembered? Did he know the truth? She felt suddenly sick.

''Amy?'' he asked. ''Are you my wife?'' The question seemed wrung out of him.

Her hands were shaking. She couldn't keep this up. She hated this whole charade.

''No,'' she heard herself say. ''No, I'm not your wife.''

CHAPTER TEN

THE silence that followed her words seemed endless, vibrating with an ominous energy that prickled along her skin. And all that time he stared at her as if in shock.

"You were pretending," he said finally, his voice desolate. "All this time you were pretending."

She shrank under his regard, feeling small and dishonest. "Michael, I had no choice, I—"

He leaped to his feet, towering over her. "Why?" he asked harshly. "Why, Amy?"

She swallowed nervously, forcing herself to meet his gaze. "You needed help, and you—"

"Help?" he exploded. "You deceived me! Is that helping? I lost my memory and you lied to me about what my reality is! You lied about the most intimate, basic facts of my life! Is that supposed to help me remember the truth?"

She had never seen him so angry. She trembled with the force of it. She wanted to explain, to make him understand. "Michael, I—" Her voice faltered and the words would not come. The blaze in his eyes made her shrivel inside.

"Spare me," he ground out, turning his back on her. He stared out of the window, body rigid, hands jammed into his jeans pockets.

She huddled on the sofa, hugging herself, trembling with fear as she stared at his back, his tight shoulders, slightly bent as if to protect himself against danger.

Silence. An eternity of silence. Finally he turned around and faced her. The fire had died in his eyes and the desolation left there made her heart contract.

"You'll need to explain some things to me," he said, his voice toneless.

"I know."

"You're not my wife, but you pretended to be these last few weeks." He pressed his eyes closed as pain twisted across his face. "You must have been my wife once; we must have been married—the photos, the stories…"

"Yes, oh, yes! The wedding photos, the pictures of our life on the island, everything I told you about us is true, Michael. I didn't lie about any of it." She heard the note of pleading in her voice. Pleading for what? For his love, his understanding and forgiveness?

"So…we are divorced?"

"Yes."

"When?"

She felt like a caged animal, trying to free itself, yet finding no escape. A sense of inevitability took hold of her. "A year ago."

A long silence. She heard the pounding of her own heart.

"I can't believe this,' he said with difficulty. "Why are we divorced? It doesn't make sense!"

The dark confusion in his face clutched at her heart.

"Our marriage didn't work out," she said softly. A simple statement—simple and devastating.

He shook his head as if he could not grasp what

she was saying. "What do you mean, it didn't work out? How could it not work out?"

She fought against a wash of emotion—the past pressing against her like a wall.

"You didn't...I didn't think you loved me anymore. I didn't think you wanted to be with me. We didn't spend time together anymore and I was unhappy...so I left."

His face had gone white. He closed his eyes briefly, then looked right at her. "Was I unfaithful to you?" he asked tonelessly. "Was there another woman?"

For a moment she was speechless. Another woman? Had he been worrying about that? "No, oh, no!" she said then. "You were never unfaithful, Michael!"

"Then what went wrong?"

"People fall out of love," she said miserably. "It happens, Michael."

He stared at her, slowly shaking his head. "No, it can't be true."

"Why not?" she whispered, shaken by his vehemence.

"Because I love you now! If I am anything like the man I was before, if my feelings now are even close to what I must have felt for you then, I could not have stopped loving you."

Tears swam in her eyes and she hugged herself against the aching in her chest. "I thought you did, Michael."

He stared at her bleakly. "And you stopped loving me."

She bent her head, not answering, not wanting to remember the way she had felt about him then—the anger, the resentment and finally something that came close to hate. She didn't want to feel like that about him ever again.

"And you left the island and divorced me," he went on. "Or was it a mutual decision?"

She shook her head, the shame bitter. "No. I left you."

Silence. Like a living energy, it touched her skin, shivered along her nerves.

He rubbed his forehead. "The dream," he said suddenly, "the dream I had in Los Angeles was actually true. You left me a note, didn't you?"

"Yes." The word was barely a whisper.

A muscle jerked in his left cheek. "And you wrote I wasn't the man you married and you didn't love me anymore."

She nodded wordlessly, tears sliding silently down her cheeks. She wiped at them with her hand. "I'm sorry, so sorry." How had it been possible for her to write those words? She had loved him. She loved him now.

"Where did you go?" he asked.

"Philadelphia. I went back to teaching high school."

"And then you heard about my accident and you came here."

"Yes."

He studied her. "Why? If you didn't love me anymore?"

She saw herself sitting in her apartment, listening on the phone to an almost hysterical Melissa pleading with her.

"Melissa called me and told me what had happened. She was terribly upset because she couldn't go to you herself and you wouldn't come to her in Boston and there wasn't anybody else to help you. So she asked me.'' She was saying it all wrong; she could tell by his expression. ''I wanted to help, Michael. I wanted to see if I could help you get your memory back.''

''Thank you,'' he said stiffly. ''And why did you lie about us being married?''

''Oh, Michael...'' She made a helpless gesture. Did he not know? Could he not guess? ''If I had told you we were divorced, would you have let me stay?''

His mouth curved ruefully. ''No, I wouldn't.'' Again he combed his fingers through his hair, looking utterly weary, looking as if he wished he were somewhere else.

She longed to wrap her arms around him, tell him she loved him, but intuition told her he wouldn't welcome this now.

''I've had the feeling all along something wasn't right,'' he said dully. ''I don't know what to think or do about this now, but I'm tired and tomorrow is another day.'' He started across the room. ''I'll sleep in the guest room.''

She jumped to her feet. ''Michael, please, don't do this!'' Once before they'd started sleeping apart, and it had been the beginning of the end.

His mouth twisted crookedly. ''I don't want any more games of pretense, Amy. There's no need.''

The words were like a slap in the face and she winced. ''Michael...'' But he was already on his way out of the room. Her stomach churning, she followed him into the master bedroom, where he gathered up some of his things.

"Michael, please," she said thickly.

He didn't look at her. "I can't deal with this right now. I need to be alone."

She watched in numb despair as he strode out of the bedroom and disappeared into the guest room at the far end of the hall.

Michael tossed his things on a chair and stood in front of the window staring out over the dark woods. He would not sleep, but he needed to be alone, away from Amy and her wide green eyes full of incomprehensible emotions. He needed desperately to sort out his thoughts and feelings, to somehow make sense out of his life.

What life? he thought bitterly. His past was an empty darkness and his future seemed hollow and meaningless.

His teeth and jaws ached. Something inside him—his soul, his pride—felt battered and bruised.

She'd felt sorry for him.

The thought was unbearable, spreading poison through his system. He swung around and leaned against the wall and pounded it with his fist. Damn, damn! He didn't want her pity, or anyone else's for that matter.

All this time she'd been playing a game—pretending she was his wife, pretending she loved him. It was a bitter truth, and it made him feel like a damned fool to have been taken in so easily.

But it explained a lot of things. He'd wondered why in the beginning she had seemed so hesitant...reluctant to show him affection. If she had truly been his wife, if she had loved him...

He pushed himself away from the wall, dropped

himself on the edge of the bed and buried his face in his hands.

She hadn't loved him. Not anymore. She'd come to help him because Melissa had been distraught and had begged her, because she felt sorry for him. He could not bear the thought, nor the memories of their lovemaking. He loved her and he'd thought she loved him back.

And it had all been a lie.

It was later in the night as he lay awake that thoughts of Jennifer Casey intruded into his mind. And the realization came to him that whatever there had been between them had not made him a cheating husband. He felt a powerful sense of relief, followed by a tidal wave of anger. All the guilt he'd secretly been carrying around with him had been unfounded and unnecessary.

He remembered Jennifer's face when he'd told her he didn't want to continue the relationship, and he thought of the e-mails she had sent him and to which he had not responded. She had not deserved the way he had treated her and he felt remorse thinking about his coolness, the hurt in her eyes.

As soon as the sun rose, he got up and went for a long run on the beach. He ran and ran and ran as if the devil himself was after him. His life was a mess and he felt out of control. He needed desperately to do something, anything, to start straightening it out.

Back in the house he showered and dressed. Amy was in the kitchen, looking as if she hadn't slept much either. She reached for the coffee pot, but he held up his hand. "I'll have some at the office," he said.

"Don't you want breakfast?"

"No, thank you." He always had breakfast, but all he could think of now was to get out of the house as fast as possible.

"Michael, please," she said. He tried not to hear the unhappiness in her voice.

"I'll see you later," he said, and strode out the door.

"Mrs. Applegate," he said to his secretary later that morning. "Do you remember Jennifer Casey who came to see me a few weeks ago? Did she leave a card?"

Mrs. Applegate riffled through her Rolodex. "Here you go, sir." She handed him a business card. "Would you like me to make a call?"

He glanced down at the card. "No, I'll do it." He went back into his office, sat down and picked up the phone. He dialed the office number in Seattle.

"My name is Michael DeLaurence and I'd like to speak to Jennifer Casey, please," he told the receptionist who answered the phone. "Is she in the country?" For all he knew she could be on a job in Poland or Thailand.

"Just came back yesterday," said the woman breezily. "One moment, please."

"Michael! I'm so glad you called." Jennifer's voice was cheerful and sincere. "How are you?"

"Well, apart from not knowing who I am, I'm fine," he said dryly.

"No progress, then?" she asked.

"I'm afraid not. But I'm beginning to piece things together and...well, to come to the point, I would like to talk to you. Are you free for dinner tonight?"

"Yes, yes, of course. Where are you?"

"In my office, but I'll take a flight out this afternoon. If you can tell me where I can reach you early this evening, I'll give you a call after I get to my hotel."

A slight pause, or maybe he imagined it. "I'll be at home." She gave him the number. "I'll look forward to seeing you, Michael."

He had Mrs. Applegate clear his schedule for the afternoon, make a reservation for a flight to Seattle and book him a room in a hotel. After lunch he went back to the house and found Amy pulling weeds in a flowerbed. They had hired the services of a landscaping company and he had no idea why she was doing that.

"Something came up," he said before she could ask why he was home. "I'm going to Seattle and I'll be back in the morning."

He changed his clothes and packed an overnight bag.

"Michael." Amy stood in the door to the bedroom watching him with sad green eyes. "Don't withdraw from me. Please talk to me."

He went on with his packing. "Right now I need some space," he said, not looking at her.

"I know you're angry with me, Michael, and I'm sorry."

He didn't know what came over him, but suddenly he could no longer keep calm. "Yes, I'm angry," he said tightly. "You didn't tell me the truth and because of that I've been running around with a pile of guilt the size of Mount Fuji, thinking I'm a lousy husband who doesn't deserve you. Oh, yes, I'm angry!"

She stared at him, wide-eyed. "Guilty about what? Why were you thinking you were a bad husband?"

"Because I thought I'd been having an affair behind your back."

She looked stunned. She clasped her hands together. "You mean...there was...is another woman?"

"Yes. But I didn't meet her until about six months ago. At least that's what she told me."

Amy swallowed visibly. "You've seen her, then?"

"Yes, once. She came to my office last month, soon after you arrived. She told me and there was no reason not to believe her." Amy looked as if he'd hit her with a brick.

"Did you meet her on the island? Do I know her?"

"You don't know her."

"Do you...want her?" she whispered, and he saw the naked terror in her eyes.

"I don't even know her! I don't remember her, or anything about our relationship. All I've been feeling is guilt, thinking I'd betrayed you, and wondering what kind of man I am to cheat on my wife." He zipped the bag closed and lifted it off the bed. "I've been trying to piece my life together and now I find that all the pieces are *wrong*. You'll forgive me if I have a little trouble adjusting."

Through the window he saw the Aurora car drive up to the house, coming to take him to the airport.

Amy knew she was losing her mind. All she could think of was the other woman. She had no name, no

picture, no idea of who she was. She had never before had any reason for jealousy and now the fear
was so thick in her throat she could taste it. Where
was this woman now? If she wanted Michael, why
wasn't she with him?

She called Melissa and told her everything.

"He never mentioned her," Melissa said, sounding bewildered. "He never mentioned any other
woman! Oh, Amy, I'm so sorry!"

"Would you do something for me?"

"Sure, if I can."

"I want to know who she is, Melissa, I want to
know *where* she is. Will you please make some calls
to the island? Talk to Sasha, or Katrina, see if you
can find out if anybody knows who she is." Melissa
had visited them on the island several times, knew
their friends.

"Are you sure you want to do this, Amy?"
Melissa sounded worried. "What will you do if I
find out?"

"I don't know...I haven't thought about it yet,
but I do want to know."

Melissa sighed. "All right, I'll try."

She called back the next morning. "I talked to
Matt at the hospital," she said. "Her name is
Jennifer Casey. She's a consultant and has worked
on the hospital computer systems. She works for a
company in Seattle. I have the name and number
here. You have a pen?"

Amy's heart was racing. "Yeah. What's her
name?"

"Jennifer Casey."

Amy's hand froze above the paper, clutching the

pen. She knew that name. Michael had mentioned it to her only days ago.

"Amy? Are you there?"

"Yes, yes, sorry. What's the name of the company?"

She wrote down what Melissa told her, then thanked her and hung up.

Amy stared at the piece of paper. Then she picked up the phone again and booked a flight for Seattle.

Amy stared at the woman standing behind the desk. She had gorgeous hair, beautiful eyes, and a friendly smile.

"Please have a seat," she said. "Would you like some coffee, tea?"

"No, thank you." Amy sat down.

"You wanted to talk to me about Michael DeLaurence," Jennifer said, sitting down again.

"Yes…" Her voice sounded odd. "I think I should tell you who I am."

"I already know," said Jennifer, and gave a faint smile. "You're Michael's wife. Or rather, ex-wife." Her voice was perfectly even, radiating no threat or hostility.

"He told you about me?"

"Yes. We had dinner last night. Didn't he tell you?"

Amy felt dazed. So that was where he had gone. "No…he…I left before he came back home…" It was hard to breathe. She felt herself shrinking into the chair.

"Why did he come to see you?" she whispered.

"He wanted to know the truth about our relationship, and to apologize because he more or less sent me away when I came to see him a few weeks ago.''

"What did he tell you about me?"

"Not very much, just that you had come to be with him after his accident." Jennifer came to her feet and sat down on the sofa next to her. "Listen to me, Amy." There was an urgent tone to her voice. "Let me tell you about him and me."

"I don't want to know."

"Yes, you do. We met on the island. He told me he was divorced. He never told me what had happened, or any details about your marriage." She took a deep breath. "We spent time together. We..." She paused.

"I lost my husband about a year and a half ago," she said then, and the look on her face expressed a world of grief.

"I'm sorry," Amy whispered.

Jennifer stared down at her hands, clasped in her lap. "I met Michael at a dinner party at Matt and Sasha's. I'm sure you know them."

Amy nodded. "Yes."

"In a nutshell, we liked each other. I was lonely; he was lonely. It was enough for a while. We... understood each other." She gave a half-smile. "I've thought about it a lot lately and I didn't really see it clearly until just recently. What we had wasn't, and isn't, a good basis for a long-term commitment." She met Amy's eyes unblinkingly. "I told Michael this last night."

Amy forgot to breathe for a moment, felt relief wash over her. "What did he say?"

Jennifer smiled again. "Something to the effect that he took my word for it because he doesn't remember a thing about any of it. I could tell he was relieved. I don't think he wants me as a complication in his life.''

Amy didn't know what to say. She had never met a woman more generous than Jennifer.

''Why are you telling me all this?'' she asked.

''Because it's the truth. And because I like Michael and I wish him the best.''

Amy was back home before dark, but Michael was not there. Before she'd gone to the airport that morning, she'd left a message with his secretary telling him she would be home late. She assumed he was out having dinner or still working at the office. She had a shower and went to bed.

For the next two days she hardly saw him. He was hiding again and avoiding her, just as he had done on the island.

The third evening she found him in the master bedroom, taking some more clothes out of his closet. He gave her a quick, sideways glance, then focussed on the clothes in front of him.

''Since you're not my wife,'' he said in the cool, collected voice of a stranger, ''you should go back to your own life.''

His words felt like a punch in the chest. She drew in a shaky breath of air. ''I don't want to.''

Even if she had wanted to, it was too late. She had no life to go back to.

He studied her, his expression inscrutable. ''I don't want your pity. I don't want you to...cater to me because you feel you have to, out of some sort of misplaced duty.''

The heat of indignation rose to her cheeks. ''Is

that what you think I'm feeling for you? *Misplaced duty?*"

He dragged out a shirt and tie and tossed them on the bed. "What I think, what I *know*, is that you deceived me," he said roughly, not looking at her. "You pretended to be what you weren't. Apart from that, how in hell am I supposed to know how to feel? What to think?" He threw a pair of socks on the bed and met her eyes. "How am I supposed to know what's real and what's not?" He turned away from her, catching sight of his own reflection in the dresser mirror.

She watched him staring at himself, something wild and dangerous in his eyes. For a frozen moment an ominous stillness trembled around them. Then he took a vicious swing with his right arm and smashed his fist through the mirror.

It shattered, spewing glass everywhere.

She cleaned up the glass after Michael had stormed out the room. It took a long time to gather up all the sharp shards of broken mirror, to search the corners and sweep under the bed. Somehow this exercise calmed her and she felt a quiet resolve settle over her.

After she was finished, she found Michael in the kitchen. He was making a sandwich for himself. They had not shared a meal in the last few days; he'd made sure of that.

She faced him squarely. "I'm not leaving," she stated, jamming her hands on her hips. "You can go ahead and smash every wretched mirror and window in this house and I'm *not* leaving."

He put the cheese slicer down and said nothing, his jaws clamped together.

"I made you a promise a few days ago," she went on, her voice steady. "I promised I would never leave you and I meant it then and I mean it now."

She watched his hand, clenched into a fist, resting beside the plate on the counter. He looked right into her eyes.

"I won't hold you to it. I don't need any favors; I don't *want* any favors."

"And certainly not from an ex-wife," she added, trying not to feel the sting of his words.

"Right." He opened the refrigerator and fished out a can of beer. He popped it open and took a drink, not bothering with pouring it into a glass. He was trying to dismiss her. She wasn't going to let him do it. She gripped the back of a chair and braced herself.

"I came here out of my own free will. And I intend to stay out of my own free will."

"I'm impressed," he said caustically. "May I remind you that two years ago you *left* me out of your own free will?"

She took in a tremulous breath, trying to control the impulse to counter his accusation with a hurtful remark of her own. She didn't want to go there; it would only make everything worse.

He tossed back another gulp of beer, then slammed the can onto the counter, slopping the brew over the edge. "And you haven't even given me a reason that makes any damn sense to me! Why did you think I didn't love you anymore? What had I done to you? Tell me!"

Not like this, she thought miserably. Not with all the anger emanating from him. The moment was wrong, all wrong. Her legs began to tremble and she tightened her grip on the back of the chair. "We drifted apart, Michael," she said desperately. "We didn't spend time together anymore and we were both unhappy. You were always working." It was all true, but it wasn't the answer to his question, yet the words kept pouring out of her mouth as if the sheer volume of them would convince him. "We didn't know how to talk to each other anymore. We didn't...we didn't even make love anymore. Our marriage had...it had completely disintegrated and I...I just had to get away. It hurt too much, Michael."

His face was all hard angles, his jaw tense. There was no love or gentleness in his expression. "Melissa must have done quite a number on you to make you want to come back here after all that," he said coldly. "How did she do it? Make you feel guilty? Make you feel sorry for poor lonely Michael with nobody to help him?"

She cringed at the sarcasm in his voice. "No! Michael, please! That's not how it was! That's *not* what I was thinking!"

"Really? Then what exactly were you thinking?"

"I don't know. I...I wasn't thinking at all. I just did it."

"You just did it," he repeated, as if to test the words.

"I...I had to."

"You *had* to?" Mockery in his voice now. "Who forced you?"

She shook her head. "That's not how I meant it,

Michael. I was…compelled. I didn't rationalize it. You needed help, so I came. I wasn't *thinking* at all!''

The truth was simple. She could see it very clearly now. She had not acted out of pity or duty. She had acted out of love, instinctively.

She closed her eyes for a moment, gathering courage. ''I came because…because I never stopped loving you. Deep down I never stopped.''

''But you walked out on me just the same,'' he said harshly. ''You damned well *divorced* me!'' The words hung like poison in the air and she had no defense—not against the words, not against his anger.

''Yes. I shouldn't have, but I did.'' *Because I couldn't bear living with you anymore. I couldn't bear the pain. I had to leave.*

Because you didn't speak to me anymore. Because you pretended nothing was wrong when everything was falling apart. Because you couldn't help me when I was dying inside. Because every time I wanted to talk, you walked away from me.

We had a baby, she wanted to shout. *We had a little girl, Michael! And she died. She was only three months old and she just died, just like that. We found her in the morning in her crib, still and cold. Do you remember, Michael? Do you remember now how I screamed for you and how we held her and rocked her and she wouldn't wake up? Do you remember?*

Her heart was pumping in wild agony. She had to get away from him and the truth she couldn't tell him—not now with his anger and bitterness corroding the atmosphere.

She tore out of the room, into the bedroom, locking the door behind her. She sagged down on the edge of the big bed, hugging herself, rocking. *Please, God,* she prayed silently. *Please, God, make it stop hurting.*

She lay awake for hours, alone in the big bed, as Michael's furious accusation echoed in her mind. *"You damned well divorced me!"*

He was angry, and wounded to the depths of his soul because he had trusted her and she had deceived him.

And, worst of all, he doubted her love for him.

"I don't care how angry he is," she said out loud into the darkness. "I don't care what he says or does. I love him."

I love him, I love him. The refrain played in her head as the hours stretched and sleep would not bless her with oblivion.

She had to convince him, show him. She would not allow him to push her away, to shut her out. Not again.

She felt a sudden, reckless determination, sat up, swung her legs over the side of the bed and came to her feet.

CHAPTER ELEVEN

HE LAY on his back, his head turned away from her. The windows were wide open, the curtains not drawn. Cool night air filled the room with the fertile scents of damp earth and growing green and pungent pine. The breeze caressed her skin as she let her nightgown slide to the floor. She slipped into the bed, the sheets cool against her body. He shifted a little, turning his head toward her, sleeping restlessly. She lay very still, gazing at the moon hanging ripe in the sky, trying to calm her racing pulse. It wouldn't slow down.

She inched closer and turned on her side. Gently she moved her body up against his, resting her head on his shoulder. His skin was warm against hers and a glow spread through her. She placed her hand on his chest, over his heart. He made a soft sound in his sleep, freeing his arm to draw her closer.

"Michael, I love you," she whispered.

He stirred, mumbling something, and relaxed back into sleep. She lay there for a while, savoring his warmth and his scent, feeling the steady drumming of his heart under her hand, knowing with soul-deep certainty that she loved him and would love him forever.

"Michael?"

"Mmm? What?" he muttered, still not conscious.

"I love you." Her voice trembled.

His arm tightened around her and he gave a soft,

166

contented sigh. "I love you too," he murmured, the words barely audible.

She felt a surge of emotion—relief, tenderness and an indescribable joy. She wanted to kiss him, to make love to him, to show him her love was real.

Then he moved, turning on his side. "Amy?"

He was awake; she could tell by the sound of his voice, the slight disbelief in his tone.

She lifted her head and looked down at his face in the faint silvery light of the moon. "Close your eyes," she whispered, and lowered her mouth to his. She kissed him softly, and he reacted with a hunger that shook her.

Fire, need. He wanted her. Sweet exultation warmed her blood.

He gave a soft groan, suddenly drawing away a little. "Amy?"

"Yes?"

"What are you doing here?" he asked, as if the reality of the situation had only just occurred to him.

"I want to make love," she said softly. "I need you, Michael, I love you."

"Amy..." A world of yearning trembled in his voice.

She searched for one of his hands and clasped it tightly. "I never pretended or faked or played games when we made love, Michael. Never. I wanted you. I always wanted you." Her voice quavered. "You know that. You have to know that."

A sigh, deep and relieved. "Yes," he muttered. "Yes, I know." He drew her to him, on top of him, and she lay there feeling all of him against her, feeling his breath on her cheek, feeling his arm heavy around her back. Feeling love.

He had not pushed her away, had not told her he didn't want her in his bed. She felt almost giddy with relief.

"I was angry with you," he mumbled. "I don't like being angry with you because I love you."

A sweetness bloomed inside her. "I know," she said softly. "It's all right."

His eyes were closed. "You're not leaving," he said sleepily.

"No, I'm not leaving." She began to kiss him, slowly at first, then more deeply, urgently, stirring him into greater wakefulness, his response coming easily and hungrily. She moved her hands over him, reveling in the feel of him, the taste of him, delighting in her intimate knowledge of his body.

"Amy..." he groaned

"Shh, shh—don't talk, don't move. Just let me love you."

He lay back, eyes closed, and allowed her to love him. Even now it amazed her to see what her mouth and hands could do to his body, gave her secret thrills to notice his shallow breathing and the unfocussed look in his dusky golden eyes.

Until he could no longer keep still and with a groan deep in his throat he gripped her waist and rolled her over on her back. His mouth on hers was hot, his kiss deep and erotic and her blood went wild. Her control was spinning away and she let it, feeling the sweet dizziness in her head take over. She gripped his hair as he put his mouth to her breast, felt the tingling of desire spiraling through her as he teased her nipples with his tongue—first one, then the other.

She loved curling her fingers through the rich

thickness of his hair, loved the shape of his head under her hands, loved the heat of his mouth around her nipples.

There was a wildness, a hungering urgency to his lovemaking that made her pulse soar and created in her an answering abandon.

No thinking. Just feeling and being with her body and all its lush sensations. Just touching and relishing the body of the man she loved until no air was left and the world fell away in a shattering explosion of heat.

She floated for a long time, drifting along without thought in blissful languor. Until finally awareness cleared as Michael's voice meandered into her consciousness. She opened her eyes.

He was braced on one elbow, observing her with a faint smile. "I always enjoy looking at you after we've made love," he said, tracing his fingers through her hair. "You're beautiful—all flushed and soft and sated and your hair sexily messed up."

His words warmed her. "You're the one making me this way, and you're so good at it."

He leaned his face close and kissed her softly. "I love you. I don't know where the feelings come from, if I remember them, or if they're all new, but they're real."

"I'm glad," she said tremulously. "I love you too…and that's real as well." Out of nowhere came a flutter of fear. "No matter what happens, Michael, it's real. Don't forget it. Please promise me." She heard the pleading note in her voice, saw concern flit across his face.

He studied her with a puzzled frown. "Amy, why would I forget that?"

She bit her lip. "I'm scared that when you get your memory back you'll remember not loving me, remember how it was between us."

His eyes held hers, probing, searching for what he did not know. "Was it that bad?" he asked softly.

She nodded, her throat aching. "Yes," she said thickly, "it was very bad." Tears blinded her. "I want to tell you everything, but it's so hard…it hurts just to think about it and I—" Her voice broke and she covered her face with her hands.

"You don't have to tell me now," he said. "Tell me when you're ready—when we're both ready."

She lowered her hands and looked at him through tear-blurred eyes. "Oh, Michael, I said such terrible things to you and I was so wrong. And…and when you remember everything—"

He took her face between his hands, gazed into her eyes with so much love she ached with it. "You're forgetting something important," he said quietly.

"What?"

"I'll also remember how it is now, and how it was ever since you came here. My feelings for you aren't going to just disappear."

She wanted to believe it desperately. "I don't want you to stop loving me ever again," she said, her voice thick.

He kissed her fiercely. "I won't. I promise I won't."

But the fear stayed with her. And the knowledge that she could not wait much longer to tell him about the baby. She owed him that.

*   *   *

The next afternoon Amy sat on the big bed, legs tucked up against her yogi-style, the baby album in front of her.

Her stomach churned; it had churned all morning knowing she had to do this, yet postponing it hour after hour. She wiped her damp forehead with her right hand.

Don't think, don't feel! Just do it!

She made herself open the album to the first page.

She was seeing herself, nine months pregnant, her belly impossibly huge. She was smiling, her face bright and happy.

Somehow her hand moved, turned the pages one by one, energized by a force outside herself.

Pictures of Lizzie only minutes old. A close-up of her tiny face against Amy's breast, nursing. Pictures of her in the pink tub, smiling. A snapshot of the three of them sitting in the love-nest chair, Lizzie in Michael's lap, so tiny in his big, strong arms.

She caught the glimmer of silver on his chest. He was wearing the sailboat disc.

Lizzie had been conceived one glorious day when they'd been sailing out in the ocean under an azure sky. Amy had known the date exactly, due to both calculation and feminine intuition. She'd had the pendant made as a present for Michael, to remember the magic of that day. The significance of the date inscribed on the back was a secret to all but the two of them.

Her hand turned another page, but Amy couldn't see anymore. The photos blurred in front of her as the tears overflowed. She could still feel the weight of Lizzie in her arms, still smell the sweet baby smell of her, still feel her tiny mouth suckling at her breast.

No more, no more.

She struggled to her feet, rushed blindly out of the house, into a drenching summer rain, not caring, only barely feeling the wetness soaking her clothes as she stumbled through the woods.

On the fringes of her consciousness she knew she was running again, always running away, and that she had to stop. She could not run forever, because she could never run far enough. The memories would be inside of her forever, no matter where she was. There was no escape.

Stop, stop. Turn back.

She slowed her pace, breathing hard.

Call Michael and tell him to come home.

She stood still, feeling the rain mingling with the tears on her face. For a long time she simply stood there listening to the sound of the rain falling on the trees around her and a stillness came over her. Her tears stopped flowing, her body calmed.

She traced her way back to the house, surprised to find herself so far away. She shivered, feeling suddenly cold in her wet clothes.

The back door was open, as she must have left it when she'd run out of the house. She took off her sodden sandals and tiptoed, dripping water, to the bedroom.

A sound caught her attention, an awful, strangled sound that made her stomach lurch in fear.

The next instant she saw Michael on his knees in front of the bed, bent over the photo album, shoulders heaving.

CHAPTER TWELVE

SHE grew utterly still as she watched Michael, his strong body convulsed with weeping. The tortured sounds seemed torn from his soul and wrenched at her heart. Instinct took over and she rushed into the room, knelt down behind him on the floor and wrapped her arms around him.

"It's all right, Michael. It's all right." She didn't know why she came up with those words—nothing that had happened was all right. All she felt was the overwhelming need to ease his distress, to give him comfort. He turned in her arms, pressing his face against her hair and clung to her.

"Oh, God," he said hoarsely, "I remember now. I remember everything."

She tried not to feel the fear slithering through her, prayed for strength and the wisdom to find the right words to say.

"I loved her," he said brokenly, "I loved her so."

"I know, I know." Tears flooded her eyes and a sob broke loose and then she was crying too.

They clung to each other, rocking, holding on.

Holding onto each other.

"You're soaked through," he said later, much later. They were still sitting on the floor, arms still around each other, like shipwreck victims stranded on a desert island. Amy felt drained, her body limp and boneless. She shivered suddenly, feeling the clammy coldness of her rain-drenched clothes against her skin.

"I ran out. I was looking at Lizzie's pictures and I couldn't take it anymore." Another shiver ran through her.

"Come on," he ordered, grasping her hands. His voice sounded normal again. He pulled her to her feet and propelled her into the bathroom. He turned on the shower, helped her take off her sodden jeans, T-shirt and underwear and guided her under the water as if she were a helpless child. Then he stripped off his own clothes.

They stood under the water together, pressing close, stroking, touching. Amy felt warmth return to her body, felt the water streaming over her like a balm, a blessing.

Michael took her face in his hands, kissed her softly. "I missed you," he said huskily. "Oh, Amy, I missed you so."

"I'm sorry," she choked out. "I'm so sorry for hurting you, for saying those terrible things to you and—"

"Shh." His lips brushed over hers to silence her. "It's all right, it's all right," he whispered against her mouth. "It was all a terrible nightmare. I love you. I never stopped loving you."

She couldn't speak; her throat ached with the effort not to cry again. His hands roamed over her, down her shoulders, her breasts, her hips, as if feeling her shape, remembering, and reveling in it. "You're my wife," he said softly, love and wonder mingling in his voice—and an unspoken question.

Relief surged through her. There was only one

response, simple and wonderful. "Yes," she whispered, meeting his eyes that had darkened a dusky gold with emotion.

"And you came back to me." His voice was unsteady.

"Yes."

"You came because you still loved me and I needed you." His voice held a sense of wonder, as if he were amazed such a thing was possible.

She gave a tremulous smile. "Yes."

He kissed her again, his face and mouth wet, his body slippery against hers. He turned off the water and led her out of the shower. Taking a towel, he began to dry her, then dried himself.

He tossed back the bedcovers and they lay down, holding each other close. It was the most wonderful, joyous feeling.

"It's been such a long time," he said.

They'd made love only the night before, but she knew what he meant and she nodded.

"Such a long time since I last made love to you knowing who you are, really knowing you're my wife." His kiss was infinitely tender, as if she were something delicate and precious.

She opened up to him, floating away in the magic of renewed loving. Their breath mingled, their bodies melded and all that existed was the two of them together, dancing the intimate dance of love... healing the past, affirming the present.

Amy lay with her head on his chest, her legs tangled with his, not wanting to let go.

They talked as darkness gathered in the room, talked about the baby in soft voices, saying all the things that needed to be expressed, no longer hiding or holding back.

"I felt like such a failure," said Michael, wrestling with the words. "I was not man enough to protect my own child from harm; I was not man enough to help you when you needed me most. I couldn't rescue you. You needed support and comfort and I couldn't give it you."

She pressed closer into him. "You're only human, Michael. You were struggling with your own grief."

"I tried not to feel it."

"But you did." He had tried to suppress it, hide behind work and activity. And then he would come home and all she wanted to do was talk and cry and talk and cry and he had felt more and more like a failure. He didn't want to talk about the baby; it hurt too much. He wanted the memories and the pain compartmentalized in a separate part of his mind to protect himself. She placed her hand on his chest, over his heart.

"I never saw you cry," she said softly.

"I cried," he said evenly. "Just never when you were around."

"Oh, Michael."

He stroked her hair. "I didn't want you to see me."

"You thought I'd think you were weak?"

"Yes. No. I... You were falling apart and I couldn't afford to fall apart too. I had to be tough, to be strong."

"And I thought you didn't care." It hurt to say the words, to admit out loud she had failed him, too.

"You told me that." The distress in his voice was not concealed.

She lifted her face to his. "I'm so sorry," she whispered. "I didn't understand, Michael."

"She was my baby, my child," he said softly. "How could you possibly think I didn't care?"

The guilt was bitter in her mouth. "I didn't understand your behavior, Michael. I was crazy with my own grief and I misinterpreted everything." She took a shaky breath. "I felt so lonely," she said on a low note. "You were…seemed so distant, Michael. I couldn't reach you. You wouldn't talk to me about the baby and I became angrier and angrier at you. I know it was wrong, but I just didn't understand it then."

"And I didn't understand your need to keep talking about what had happened. All I wanted was *not* to talk about it." He closed his eyes briefly. "There was a lot we didn't understand about each other," he said slowly.

She drew herself up, bracing herself on one elbow, and looked at him. "That's not so strange is it? How were we supposed to understand how to cope with losing our baby? How can anyone make sense out of something that horrible? How can we even know how to help each other when we don't know how to deal with it ourselves?"

"Yes." He took in a long unsteady breath. "Amy, we should have found help. We made a terrible mistake by allowing everything to deteriorate to the point of no return."

"I know." She swallowed. "I should never have left you, never walked out on our marriage."

"And I should have come after you, made you

come back. I should never have allowed you to divorce me." He shifted his body, reached out and drew her tight against him. "I'm never letting you go again."

Her heart flowed over with love, with the miracle of being with him again, being loved by him. She lowered her face to his chest, felt the solid beat of his heart against her cheek.

They were silent for a while. "You found the book about grieving," she said then. "You read it, didn't you?"

"Yes. I never knew we had it. I found it on the island when I was packing up. I sat down and read it straight through."

Amy sighed. "Somebody had sent it to me and I was so furious at the implication that a stupid *book* could offer any help that I never read it, not until just a couple of weeks ago when I found it again in one of the boxes."

He adjusted the pillow under his head. "It's a good book," he said.

"I know." She lifted her face. "You know, I never read any self-help books, never thought much about them, but then I never really needed help before. It's easy to be arrogant when you think you know everything."

He laughed softly, putting a warm hand on her hip. "You're not arrogant. I'd never love an arrogant woman."

"Well, you know what I mean."

"I know what you mean." He stroked her hip. "You know what it said about divorce in the book? Seventy-five percent of couples who lose a child end up divorcing."

"I never thought of myself or our marriage as a statistic."

"It's sobering to look at it that way."

"I don't like it," she said, sounding like a stubborn child.

He gave a half-smile. "You know what we'll do?"

She shook her head.

"We'll get married again. If you agree, of course."

She frowned. "That doesn't sound right."

He cocked a brow. "It doesn't?"

"We already got married once, and there was nothing wrong with that. What was wrong was the divorce. What I really want is to annul the divorce. Do you suppose we can do that?"

He laughed. "I doubt it, but we can certainly find out."

"And if that doesn't work, we'll get married again quietly, just the two of us, nobody else there."

"Anything you want."

She let out a deep sigh. "There's something else I want you to know."

"What?"

"I know about Jennifer Casey. I didn't when you asked me," she added hastily, "but I found out later."

She told him everything and he listened without saying a word.

"She's a very special person," Amy said finally.

"Yes, she is. And we never loved each other, just as she told you."

"I was terrified that you did," Amy admitted.

He gave a crooked smile. "So was I, but I don't

need to worry about it anymore, because now I know. The only woman I ever loved is you.''

"Please keep reminding me," she muttered, and rested her face against his chest. She closed her eyes and images and thoughts and memories danced through her mind. "Michael?"

"Mmm. What?"

"What did you do with Lizzie's things? Her crib, her clothes?"

"I gave them to the orphanage. Sasha suggested it. Do you mind?"

"No, of course not. It was a great idea." It was good to think they would be used in a place they were needed. She was silent for a few minutes. "There's something else," she said then. She hesitated, wondering if maybe this wasn't the time, but if this wasn't, then when? Her pulse did a nervous little dance. She moistened her lips. "Michael, do you want us to have another baby?"

She felt him grow still against her. "Only if you want to."

"I do. I do want another baby, I want it so much it hurts, but it scares me too."

"Because of what happened." His voice was low, colored with the pain of memory.

"Yes." Would they ever dare close their eyes at night again with a new baby sleeping nearby?

Michael reached up to touch her face. "We'll go to the experts. We'll get advice. We'll figure it out, Amy; we'll do it together."

Together.

A beautiful word, she thought, a word full of promise and strength. "Nothing is ever going to come between us again,'' she said, her voice catching with emotion.

He touched her cheek. "We won't allow it."

The rain had stopped and into the silence came the exquisite fluting of a bird, a triumphant exultant affirmation of life. They listened to it wordlessly, holding each other.

"Do you remember," Michael asked after a while, "that I said I had the feeling that there was a reason for what was happening to me? A reason I'd had the accident, a reason I couldn't remember you, couldn't remember my life?"

She rubbed her face against his chest. "Yes, I do."

"I think I was right. I think it was meant to happen so we could find each other again. To give us another chance to love each other all over again."

She found herself smiling. "It wasn't very hard."

He was smiling too. "I might not have recognized you as my wife, but the moment I saw you at the airport I *knew* I loved you."

She remembered putting her arms around him, remembered recognizing the familiar feel of him, his scent, his warmth. Remembered breaking into tears.

"Me too," she whispered.

EPILOGUE

MICHAEL opened the front door and put his briefcase on a chair in the entryway The house was quiet. Loosening his tie, he strode into the living room and found it empty. Glancing out the large windows, he saw Amy and Timmy sitting in the grass in the back-yard. They were absorbed by something in front of them, a cricket maybe, or a beetle. Timmy was en-chanted by every creepy crawly that came his way.

They made a lovely picture, the young woman and the small boy. My wife, he thought, my son. He stood for a few moments, just enjoying the little scene. Amy's hair was long, shimmering gold in the sunlight. Timmy's was dark, like his own, but he had his mother's green eyes.

At times like these, Michael could not believe his own good fortune. What more could a man want than to come home to a wife and child he loved?

He threw his tie and jacket on a chair and stepped out of the sliding glass doors onto the wooden deck and into the yard. They both looked up as they heard him. Timmy leaped to his feet and came running toward him on his sturdy brown legs, his face bright with excitement.

''Daddy! Come and see!'' He grasped Michael's hand and tugged at it, his little fingers warm and sticky.

Michael smiled down at the eager face. A smudge

of mud decorated the firm little chin. ''What did you find, buddy? A worm? A frog?''

''No, no! Come and see, Daddy!''

Michael allowed himself to be pulled to where Amy was sitting. She glanced up at him with a smile and he bent down to kiss her.

''Daddy, look!''

Michael looked. The object of his son's fascination was a turtle, slowly lumbering away from them.

''Wow!'' Michael said with appropriate enthusiasm.

''His head was inside!'' Timmy said excitedly. ''Cause he was scared! But now he's not anymore.'' He skipped ahead of the turtle, plopped himself in the grass and watched the little creature crawling toward him, his eyes full of wonder.

Michael sat down in the grass next to Amy and they both watched Timmy. ''It's a very exciting world, isn't it?'' he said with a grin. ''So many creatures to discover, so many things to enjoy.''

''Yes,'' she said, taking his hand and squeezing it. ''How about you? Did you get your share of happiness and joy today?''

''Mmm…'' He put his arm around her and drew her closer. He smelled the faint, flowery scent of her hair. ''Just coming home to both of you is pretty good.''

''Can you take some more excitement?'' she asked. ''Or would that overdose your system?''

He saw the shine in her eyes, knew she was up to something. ''Try me,'' he said.

Her face looked radiant and suddenly he knew what she was going to say and his heart filled to overflowing. ''Amy…''

"I'm pregnant," she said.

He drew her into his arms, suddenly lost for words.

"Me too!" Timmy shouted, and a moment later his little body wriggled between them.

Michael drew him into the embrace. "Okay, buddy, let's have a group hug."

And so Michael held his family—his wife, his son, and the new baby to come—and he knew his world was complete.

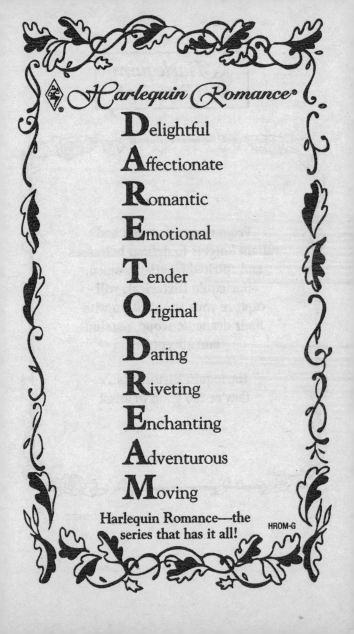

Harlequin Romance®

Delightful

Affectionate

Romantic

Emotional

Tender

Original

Daring

Riveting

Enchanting

Adventurous

Moving

Harlequin Romance—the
series that has it all!

HROM-G

Harlequin® Historical

From rugged lawmen and valiant knights to defiant heiresses and spirited frontierswomen, Harlequin Historicals will capture your imagination with their dramatic scope, passion and adventure.

Harlequin Historicals...
they're too good to miss!

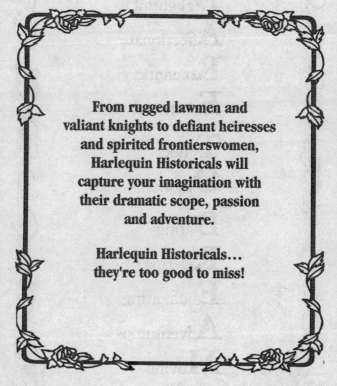

HHGENR